"I need you to kiss me, Nicholas."

Camille's whispered plea was his undoing. He couldn't have said no, couldn't have resisted if his life had depended on it.

He leaned in, let his lips brush hers. She shivered. Just a soft, chaste meeting of the lips. The sensation sent desire rushing through him.

She touched his face. Not the smooth, undamaged side, but the ugly, ravaged side. He started to draw away, but her other hand curled around his neck and held him still. Gentle fingers traced the hideous scars. He wanted to bolt, to hide his ugliness from her beauty.

"I don't see this when I look at you," she murmured. "I only see you. The man I once loved so much."

He wanted to respond, but couldn't let this distract him. Not only did Camille and her child's well-being depend on him, but the future of Raven's Cliff hung in the balance as well. He needed to remember that.

DEBRA WEBB

MOTIVE: SECRET BABY

HARLEQUIN®

TORONTO • NEW YORK • LONDON
AMSTERDAM • PARIS • SYDNEY • HAMBURG
STOCKHOLM • ATHENS • TOKYO • MILAN • MADRID
PRAGUE • WARSAW • BUDAPEST • AUCKLAND

Special thanks and acknowledgment to Debra Webb for her contribution to The Curse of Raven's Cliff miniseries.

This book is dedicated to the folks who live in small towns. I'm certain when Dorothy said those famous words, "There's no place like home," she was talking about the small towns and the folks who live there. Where life is simple and everyone knows everyone else and everyone cares.

ISBN-13: 978-0-373-88866-5
ISBN-10:   0-373-88866-X

MOTIVE: SECRET BABY

ABOUT THE AUTHOR

Debra Webb was born in Scottsboro, Alabama, to parents who taught her that anything is possible if you want it bad enough. She began writing at age nine. Eventually, she met and married the man of her dreams, and tried some other occupations, including selling vacuum cleaners, working in a factory, a daycare center, a hospital and a department store. When her husband joined the military, they moved to Berlin, Germany, and Debra became a secretary in the commanding general's office. By 1985 they were back in the States, and finally moved to Tennessee, to a small town where everyone knows everybody else. With the support of her husband and two beautiful daughters, Debra took up writing again, looking to mystery and movies for inspiration. In 1998, her dream of writing for Harlequin came true. You can write to Debra with your comments at P.O. Box 64, Huntland, Tennessee 37345, or visit her Web site at http://www.debrawebb.com to find out exciting news about her next book.

Books by Debra Webb

HARLEQUIN INTRIGUE

*Colby Agency
**The Equalizers

CAST OF CHARACTERS

Camille Wells—The mayor's missing daughter has returned, having recently given birth, and with no memory of where she has been for nearly a year.

Nicholas Sterling III (aka Ingram Jackson)—The recluse known as "the beast" has been revealed as back-from-the-dead Nicholas Sterling.

Chief Swanson—He isn't so sure Camille can't remember what happened to her baby.

Grant Bridges—He only wants to help the woman he still loves and the man he feels deserves a second chance…or does he?

Alex Gibson—Is he really dead? A number of people witnessed his plunge over the cliffs but no body was found.

Perry Wells—The former mayor appears to want what is best for his daughter.

Beatrice Wells—She wants her life back. Will the price be her daughter's sanity?

Rick Simpson—The newly elected mayor.

Prologue

The waves crashed ferociously against the rocky shore, sending a salty mist spraying over his bare back. The cool, damp sand beneath his arms felt familiar and comforting. But it was the woman in his arms that filled his heart and soul with longing, and at the same time with torment. Nicholas Sterling III stared into the eyes of the woman he held so tightly.

The woman with whom he had made slow, passionate love for the last time.

How could he never hold her this way again? How could he pretend what they shared meant nothing and go on with his life?

Agony squeezed his heart. Yet he must. He had an obligation. His family had arranged his marriage, his whole life. Starting tomorrow.

There was no way to stop the momentum. He was to marry the chosen bride and settle into his arranged future or lose everything. His family…his inheritance. To defy his family's wishes would be to exile himself from Raven's Cliff and all that he knew.

Did he not possess the courage to start over somewhere else on his own? With nothing?

Nicholas pushed away the thought. Perhaps he was a coward. It was far too late to delve into a self-analysis. Tomorrow he would do as his family demanded.

But tonight was his. His and Camille's.

One last night to hold her. Nicholas dipped his head and tasted her sweet lips once more. Camille whimpered softly. She loved him. He knew she did.

And he loved her…desperately.

Unfortunately love was not enough.

He stilled. The bitterness of regret tainted his soul despite his determination to put all but this moment aside. The truth was, what he was doing now was unfair to Camille. Unfair to the woman he was to marry and to his family.

Those damned obligations.

This was a hell of a time for his conscience to decide it worked after all. Not once had he ever let anyone else's expectations block his path, so why tonight?

What made this night different from all the others that had come before it?

Just because in less than twenty-four hours he was scheduled to wed a woman his family had handpicked for him…just because…

Doom crashed down around him as if lightning had struck with unerring force. An overwhelming sense of loss pressed against his chest.

Tonight…was *the* night.

"Dear God…" He'd forgotten to go to the lighthouse.

"What's wrong?" Camille wiggled out of his arms and scooted up to a sitting position. "Nicholas?"

His gaze met hers and in a single instant he saw his true destiny reflected there. *Death.*

"I have to go." Nicholas scrambled to his feet, jerked on his jeans. "I'm sorry. I—"

"Please tell me what's wrong." Draping her abandoned dress over her bare breasts, she stared up at him, her eyes wide with worry and sadness…with her own regret. This was their last time together.

For a moment he couldn't move. He wanted so badly to take her into his arms again…to promise her whatever necessary to banish the sadness in those blue eyes.

How had he allowed his life to come to this place where nothing was as it should be?

A deafening whoosh blasted the night air, shattering the thick, tense silence. Nicholas lifted his face to the night, scanned the craggy cliff above their secluded, sandy haven.

Flames danced, illuminating the dark velvet sky.

"The lighthouse…" Apprehension tightened its noose on his neck.

He had to hurry. Before it was too late.

Nicholas ran, skirted the rocky shore his feet knew by heart until he reached the narrow path that ascended the jagged cliff side.

His grandfather had warned him not to forget.

But Nicholas had shirked that obligation as he had most put before him.

Now he was too late.

Way too late.

The designated time had come and gone.

Dread constricted his lungs, making it difficult to breathe.

What had he done?

As he reached the summit, found his balance on the ledge that overlooked the restless ocean below, his worst fears were realized.

The lighthouse was on fire...the upper portion—the watch room where the lantern waited...*unlit*—glowed with the destructive fingers of fire.

A new kind of panic seized his heart.

"Grandfather!"

Though Nicholas had ignored his duty, his grandfather never would. Nicholas charged toward the lighthouse, flung open the door and mounted the steep, winding stairs two at a time.

"Grandfather!"

When he bounded up the final step his heart lurched. The watch room was almost completely engulfed. A kerosene can was overturned near the lantern. His grandfather lay on the floor beside it. Nicholas rushed to the motionless old man and dropped to his knees.

"Grandfather, it's okay. I'm here now." He lifted the old man into his arms.

Unseeing eyes peered up at him. Anguish tore at Nicholas's soul.

"No!" The scream echoed around him. The flames crept closer. Nicholas didn't care. His grandfather was dead and it was his fault.

"No. No. No." Desperate, Nicholas attempted CPR. "Breathe," he demanded between the puffs of air he forced into the unresponsive lungs.

Splitting glass screeched above the roar of the devouring blaze.

Nicholas glanced up at the lantern. The glass had shattered. He surveyed the wall of glass surrounding the watch room, then the floor where jagged shards had been spewed across it. The heat from the flames, he realized. The fire had swept a full circle around him.

He peered down at his grandfather. "I'm sorry," he murmured. "I'm so sorry."

Ice abruptly rushed through Nicholas's veins. His gaze was drawn back to the lantern as if a voice had whispered from it. The precious gemstones suddenly glistened, reflecting the light of the savage flames. Words gleamed across the metal of the lantern's casement—words he had never noticed before.

Fire and ice…life and death…look into your heart.

Confusion and misery made Nicholas's head spin.

He had killed his grandfather…destroyed the lighthouse…he was responsible…all of this was his fault.

Now is not the time to give up…there is still hope.

A force Nicholas could not name drew him to his feet…drew him to the lantern.

I pray the hollows my soul to keep.

Nicholas could almost hear his grandfather's voice reciting the silly childhood prayer….

His grandfather lay still, unmoving on the floor.

This didn't make sense. Nicholas was delusional. Did one lose his mind in those final moments before death claimed him?

Now I lay me down to sleep.

"Stop!" Nicholas put his hands over his ears. This couldn't be real.

I pray the hollows my soul to keep.

A frantic cry from far below snapped Nicholas from the baffling trance he'd slipped into. He coughed. Smoke had invaded deep into his lungs.

Another desperate cry.

Camille.

She shouted his name from the ground below.

If she tried to come up the stairs after him…too dangerous.

He would not be responsible for her death as well.

Summoning the courage that had deserted him in his misery, he shouted, "Get help!" Nicholas rushed back to where his grandfather lay and hefted him into his arms. He tried to dart through the flames to reach the stairs, but it was impossible. The entire upper portion of the staircase was swallowed up by the devouring blaze.

Defeat sucked at Nicholas's trembling limbs. There was no escape.

He was going to die.

Nicholas peered down at his beloved grandfather.

This was Nicholas's fault. He deserved to die.

And Raven's Cliff will die with you.

He jerked with a start at the words.

Where had that voice come from?

He turned all the way around. The fire had trapped him. Yet, there was no one else, except his grandfather, who could have spoken to him.

Nicholas shook his head. He was hearing things again. His jaw hardened as sweat ran down his bare skin. *You deserve to die,* he reminded himself and the voice.

Yes, he deserved no better than this.

Cradling his grandfather, Nicholas dropped to his knees to await his fate.

He heard the voice again. *The riddle is the key to salvation...to reversing the curse.*

Nicholas closed his eyes and shook his head. The heat...had to be the heat. He was going to die. He was imagining the voice. He didn't believe in the curse. He didn't believe in anything.

If you die...Raven's Cliff will die, too.

What the hell? Nicholas forced his eyes open and demanded, "Who are you?"

Salvation lies inside you...find it and you will stop the curse and save Raven's Cliff.

The curse. Fury roared through Nicholas

like a clawing beast. His entire life had been focused on his own selfish desires. He'd put what he considered foolish tales about the curse aside. Had laughed at his grandfather's insistence that it was real.

Now it was too late. The curse he had scoffed at was happening. Would be his legacy. Every single detail his grandfather had repeated to him time and again filtered through his churning thoughts.

Raven's Cliff would die just as his grandfather had…because of him.

Salvation lies inside you…. The words echoed inside Nicholas's head.

His attention rested on his grandfather once more. For his entire life Nicholas had been taught that Raven's Cliff's future lay with him. For the first time he understood with complete certainty that his grandfather's warnings were true.

But it was too late.…

No. Determination detonated inside him. He had to do something. To repair the damage he had done.

He surveyed the fate closing in on him.

But there was no escape.

Still, he had to try.

Eyes clenched, Nicholas kissed his grand-father's forehead before gently lowering him to the floor once more.

"I won't let you down again," he mur-mured to the man who had been his only real father.

Nicholas pushed unsteadily to his feet, slowly turned all the way around. The fire stood like a wall between him and any means of escape.

All hope will die with you, the voice urged. *Act! Act now!*

He had to do something.

Now.

But how?

Realization settled over him.

There was only one way to escape this fate.

Mentally picturing the churning waters below, Nicholas angled his body and dashed forward into the flames. He cried out as the heat charred his flesh. With an adrenaline charge providing the necessary strength, he propelled himself beyond what remained of the shattered glass wall.

Rain pelted his burning skin.

Nicholas felt himself plummeting against the buffeting wind of the coming storm.

Camille's frantic cry echoed in his ears.

And then the hungry sea swallowed him.

Chapter One

Five years later...

A beast.

Nicholas Sterling III stared at his reflection in the window a moment longer before yanking the rotting drapes closed.

There wasn't a single viable mirror in the cottage. He'd rendered each useless with black spray paint.

Useless...like his life.

The occasional glimpse he caught of himself in a window reminded him of what he was.

Of what the villagers saw when they looked at him.

Of what *she* would see....

That was why he hadn't attempted to see Camille again since she'd regained consciousness in the hospital. As long as she'd remained in a coma he'd sat by her bed for hours each night after her family had gone home. Chief Swanson had ordered his deputies to leave Nicholas be when he appeared late at night to sit with her. Twenty-four-hour security outside Camille's hospital room had been necessary despite the fact that Raven's Cliff's troubles appeared to be over.

All but one.

Nicholas had not been able to take control of his family's estate as of yet. Beacon Manor sat empty now that the Monroe family had realized the property could not be legally sold to them. But to assume control of what was rightfully his, Nicholas would be forced to reveal his identity. So far only a select few knew who he was. Chief Swanson and one of his detectives, Andrei Lagios, and Camille. She had been in a coma until recently and represented no threat to Nicholas. The others aware of his true identity had agreed that Raven's Cliff needed time to recover before facing another shock. And the revelation that Nicholas Sterling III not only lived but was back in town would not be welcome news, particularly on the heels of such devastation. First the poisoned fish, then a thwarted terrorist attack, not to mention a serial killer. The village was weary of tragedy.

The citizens of Raven's Cliff had thought Nicholas dead since that night five years ago when he'd initiated this horrific chain of events. He closed his eyes and steadied himself. All that had happened—the deaths, the damage to the village and the residents' livelihoods—had been his fault and his alone.

Nicholas had failed to carry out his one responsibility, and that careless mistake had caused so much misery.

Swanson continued to urge Nicholas to keep a low profile a bit longer. Raven's Cliff had a new mayor who was settling his constituents into a path toward recovery and a brighter future. Though it angered him on some level, Nicholas understood the chief's request. Causing more pain was not his intent.

Theodore Fisher, a lifetime resident and a man whose insanity had led him to poison the villagers with his concocted fish nutrient, had been stopped. As had the Seaside Strangler, Alexander Gibson, but not before he murdered four innocent victims. Rebecca Johnson had been his first victim. Nicholas shuddered as the tortured memories throttled him. That, too, was his fault. Had he been with Rebecca, the woman his family had chosen to be his wife, that night rather than selfishly indulging his own desires, she would not have been kidnapped and murdered.

Five years. A lifetime.

Even worse, Alexander Gibson had been Nicholas's identical twin. Ensuring the Sterling name was again synonymous with the devastation of Raven's Cliff. Nicholas and Alexander had been separated as small boys. Nicholas vaguely remembered playing with a boy who looked exactly like him, but as he'd grown up he had assumed that the identical playmate had been nothing more than his vivid imagination. But he'd been wrong. Alexander had tried to drown Nicholas in the bathtub at the tender age of four. Nicholas's parents had sent him away. But Alexander had eventually learned the truth and returned to carry out his sick vengeance on the village and the people who had banished and abandoned him.

The Sterling family, particularly Nicholas, was undeniably responsible for the horrors that had plagued Raven's Cliff for so many years.

It was time to make full restitution.

Every additional day Nicholas was forced to wait tortured him. He plowed his hands through his hair and paced the floor. Five endless years.

He had to finish setting the past to right.

For those five years the world he had once known had thought him dead, a victim of the fire that had stolen his beloved grandfather's life. In truth, Nicholas had barely survived that night. He'd thrown himself from the blazing watch room of the lighthouse and crashed into the ocean far below. When he'd awakened on the rocks miles away he had suffered death a thousand times over. At first from the burns that had disfigured the left side of his face and torso, then later from the knowledge of what he had done.

He had devastated so many lives.

Death would have been so much easier. Yet, he had realized that he, ironically, was Raven's Cliff's only hope.

Salvation lies inside you…

It was Nicholas's responsibility to restore the lighthouse and its lantern and to end once and for all the curse that had haunted Raven's Cliff for five years.

As a younger man he had scoffed at his grandfather's tales about the curse related to the lighthouse. Nicholas had refused to believe in such a ridiculous concept.

But he had been wrong.

That night, as he'd held his dead grandfather in his arms amid those lethal flames, a voice had warned him that if he died, Raven's Cliff would die as well.

Salvation lies inside you…

Bracing his hands on the mantel, Nicholas stared into the flames of the small fireplace that warmed his run-down cottage as he recalled that night in detail. A line from the prayer his grandfather had recited to him every single night of his childhood had echoed through him before he'd taken that suicidal plunge into the ocean.

I pray the hollows my soul to keep.

As a child Nicholas had often giggled at his grandfather's parody of the well-known prayer.

Now I lay me down to sleep.
I pray the hollows my soul to keep.
If I should die before I wake…

He couldn't remember the final line, but
every instinct told Nicholas that there was
more to the old bedtime rhyme than he'd ini-
tially thought. Since his return to Raven's
Cliff his instincts had prodded him to look to
the past for answers to the present's troubles.

Despite the relief the villagers felt at
having overcome the trials involving terrorists and a couple of lunatics with visions of
grandeur, there would be more suffering to
come. The troubles would not stop until
Nicholas had done his part.

He must restore the lighthouse and the
precious lantern it housed. It was the only
way to lift the curse and ensure a safe and
prosperous future for the village.

Not an easy task when he could not
reclaim his home.

A pounding at the front door jerked him
from the disturbing thoughts.

Tension rippled within his muscles. Who
would dare to show up at his door at this time

of night? No one came near the dilapidated cottage even in the light of day.

The few residents who had gotten a glimpse of him called him the beast. No one wanted to cross his path, much less pay a visit to his home.

Had Chief Swanson come with news of *her*?

A shiver of uncertainty trembled in Nicholas's limbs. She was far better off without him. Just as he had done to all those who had ever cared about him, he had damaged her life more than enough as it was. And still, great diligence was required to keep his thoughts away from her.

Camille Wells.

The woman he had once loved with all his heart. At least with all the heart he had possessed. The fact that she knew he was still alive had been an accident.

Just another grave mistake in a life filled with far too many repeat blunders. One stormy night almost one year ago Nicholas had come upon her below the cliffs…in that same place where they had last made love. He'd tried to hide but she'd seen him in the shadows. Once the initial shock had passed, they had argued fiercely. The heated fury had evolved into another kind of fire. They'd ended up making love right there in the sand as they had more than four years prior.

His traitorous body relished those forbidden memories.

Another round of frantic pounding echoed through his ramshackle home.

His brow furrowed with annoyance and no small amount of uncertainty. It was too late for Martha, his housekeeper, to have returned for any reason. Nicholas glanced at the clock. Half past eleven. She would be in bed by now.

It had to be Swanson.

And if it was, the news couldn't be good.

Had more evil struck?

Fear knotted in Nicholas's gut. Surely Camille's condition had not taken a turn for the worse. Two weeks ago she had regained consciousness and he had not returned to the hospital.

The night they had made love he had urged her to consider him dead as she had for more than four years. Her life would only be devastated further with him in it. She had let him know in no uncertain terms that she would be happy to do so. She wanted nothing to do with him.

Perhaps it had been the glimpse she'd gotten of him in the moonlight after they'd made love so savagely in the sand.

He'd seen the look of horror on her beautiful face. She'd tried to hide it, but failed. Not that he could blame her.

He was a beast.

And for a while he had hoped she intended to move on with her life. Then she'd disappeared…and he'd blamed himself. One stolen moment with him had brought misfortune to her once more.

More banging on the door.

His visitor was not going away. He turned to the door. "Go away!" he commanded. If it was anyone but the chief, that should be sufficient cause to send them running.

"Nicholas!"

The fear that had twisted his gut now morphed into outright terror.

It was *her.*

Camille.

Before he could stop the automatic reaction he was at the door, preparing to open it.

When had she been released from the hospital?

What was she doing here?

Though the immediate dangers to Raven's Cliff and all who resided there had passed, evil still lurked close by. Nicholas could feel it deep in his bones.

The curse.

Nothing would stop it…except the full restoration of the lighthouse and its precious lantern.

And only he could make that happen.

"Nicholas, I will not go away!" Camille's voice reverberated through the closed door. "Let me in! Please."

The last word trembled from her.

Something was wrong.

Unable to ignore her urgent plea, he slid back the dead bolt and opened the door.

His heart stumbled at the sight of her. He'd forgotten it was raining outside. A violent storm had come and gone, leaving in its wake a persistent and cleansing rain. Camille stood on his stoop, her clothes soaked and clinging to her shivering body. For one moment his gaze was lost to her beauty. The wet clothing formed to her skin, accenting the curves his hands, even now, longed to caress. Fool.

"I need your help," she pleaded.

His eyes met hers, and the fear there launched a new terror inside him.

"Come inside." He stood back, opened the door wider.

She stepped over the threshold, her arms hugged tightly around herself.

That treacherous uncertainty plagued him even as he knew what he should do. "I'll get you a blanket."

She started to argue but he turned his back and walked away. In the hall, he rummaged in the linen closet for a towel and a blanket. His housekeeper's work was reliable. Despite the cottage's run-down condition she worked diligently to maintain a certain level of cleanliness and orderliness.

Nicholas was grateful she did so without question. She appeared not to care who he was or what he did, only that he paid her a good wage for a good day's work. For nearly five years that had been enough.

Bracing himself, he returned to where Camille waited. She looked pale and tired.

Not well at all. Damp curls snuggled her soft cheeks, underscoring the dark circles beneath her eyes. His pulse reacted with worry and other emotions he fiercely wanted to deny.

"When were you released from the hospital?" He handed her the towel first.

She scrubbed at her face, then smoothed the terry cloth over her hair. "Two days ago."

The frown etched more deeply into his brow. "You're feeling better now?" She had teetered on the edge of death for days. He couldn't believe she'd awakened and walked out of the hospital as if death hadn't very nearly claimed her. "They determined what made you so ill?"

She clutched the towel at her breast and focused a glower on him. The vulnerability vanished, replaced by what looked like anger. "Don't pretend to care about my well-being."

He flinched at the accusation. "Of course I care about your well-being." He took the towel from her, tossed it aside, then carefully draped the blanket around her shoulders.

She stiffened at the slightest brush of his fingers. The reaction was like a kick to his midsection. But then, what did he expect?

Any tender feelings she'd had for his memory had vanished in the wake of the impact of his return…of his betrayal. He had allowed her to believe him dead.

"I need your help."

Part of him wanted to assure her that whatever she needed he would gladly provide. He'd been supporting Raven's Cliff's recovery efforts since he returned. Anonymously, of course. It was the least he could do. But helping Camille would be another tragic mistake. She wouldn't need money; her family was quite wealthy despite her father's, the former mayor's, recent fall from grace. Whatever help Camille thought she needed from him, she was wrong. He would only bring more pain to her life.

"You should go." He cleared his expression of any emotion. It would be in her best interests if he acted like the beast he appeared to be. "Coming here was a mistake."

She blinked, stood mute for a long moment as if she didn't know how to respond to his refusal.

"Your presence could give away my identity. The villagers are already overly curious and suspicious about me," he offered. He shouldn't have bothered with an explanation, but that foolish part of him that still loved her so dearly wouldn't allow the slight.

"I should have known," she snapped, something far too much like disgust in her tone and her eyes. "Of course you wouldn't want me to risk revealing the truth. You might be inconvenienced with having to explain yourself."

He clamped his jaw shut against the denial. Let her believe what she would as long as it sent her on her way.

"If my being here causes you trouble, that's too bad," she said, standing her ground. "You have to help me." She pulled the blanket more tightly around her but even that couldn't disguise the way her body trembled. "No one else will believe me."

"Stop." He couldn't deal with this. Being in the same room alone with her was difficult enough. She deserved better than him. Far better. He couldn't allow her to drag him into whatever was going on in her life. He couldn't risk hurting her again.

More important, his entire focus had to be

on gaining access to the lighthouse, on stopping whatever plague the curse would send next. He wasn't about to try to explain that to her. Even he didn't fully understand. But he knew. He *knew* what he must do.

"Camille." He swallowed, the taste of her name on his lips taking his breath. Forced away the need to touch her…to do anything she asked of him. "You cannot come here again. No one can know who I am. If someone sees you here, suspicions will be aroused and trouble will follow." He reached for the door. "Go home. Your family can help you with whatever problem you're encountering."

"No." She shook her head adamantly. "You're the only one who can help me."

Nicholas closed his eyes and struggled to maintain his composure. He could not be tempted. He could not permit himself to be drawn into her life again.

"Go home, Camille. I can't help you." He opened his eyes and leveled an icy glare on her. Whatever it took to push her away. "Go. Now."

"Someone took my baby."

Her words shook him. Shocked him.

"Baby?" Camille had a child? Then he remembered, she'd gone missing on her wedding day. The day she was supposed to have married Grant Bridges. Misery ached inside him.

She nodded jerkily. "While I was… missing." Her head moved side to side with the weight of uncertainty. "I don't remember anything. The man…" She shrugged, clearly unsure of her words. "The man who held me kept me drugged or something. I don't remember anything after falling from the cliff. All I know is that I was pregnant and now I'm not. The doctor said I'd given birth only a few weeks before I was found." She drew in a jagged breath. "My baby's missing and Chief Swanson thinks I…"

Tears welled in those big blue eyes. "Chief Swanson thinks what?" Nicholas heard himself ask, no matter that he knew with every fiber of his being that he should usher her out the door. He should not allow himself to be distracted…not even for Camille.

He'd made that mistake once. And it had cost them both far too much already.

"He thinks I did something—" she moistened her quivering lips "—with my baby. He won't help me because he thinks I did something unspeakable."

"Swanson is a reasonable man." Nicholas steeled his emotions. He could not help her. "You should talk to him again. Insist that he at least consider all avenues, including the possibility that whoever held you took your child."

The vulnerability disappeared once more. "He won't help me," she argued. "He and his men are investigating me. They're not looking for my baby." The anguish tormenting her trickled beyond the determination she attempted to exhibit. "I'll have to do this without the help of the authorities." Another big breath. "And I can't do it alone."

Enough. He had allowed this to go too far already. If he didn't send her away now he would end up agreeing to her request, and that would be a mistake for her and for him. Trouble would soon descend upon Raven's Cliff once more if he didn't complete his quest.

"I'm afraid I can't help you." He moved to the door. "Go home, Camille. You have the means to find the help you need. Hire a private investigator." He met her worried gaze once more. "You don't need me."

"No." She lifted her chin in defiance. "I need your help. There is no one else I can depend on."

Anger flared, burning away the tender emotions he had foolishly experienced. If she needed someone, she should turn to Grant Bridges. After all, she had been ready to marry him before she'd disappeared. He was assuredly the child's father. Why didn't she go to him now?

"Go to Bridges." The words ground from between clenched teeth. Nicholas hated that jealously was reflected in each word, but some part of him was obviously still human. Grant Bridges had once been his best friend. As much as Nicholas wanted to hate him for almost marrying Camille, he had no right. Camille deserved a good man, and Bridges was a good man.

"I can't."

Patience thinning, Nicholas gestured to the door once more. "I'm certain he will be glad to help you in any way you need. He was supposed to be your husband as I recall. He faithfully visited you in the hospital." Nicholas stared out the open door and into the dark night as he said the rest. "Bridges would never shirk his responsibilities. Go to him."

"You don't understand. I can't go to him." She still made no move toward the door. "You're the only person who can help me."

A muscle in his jaw jerking with tension, Nicholas moved in close to her, a blatant act of intimidation. The sweet scent of her filled his nostrils, almost defeated his determination. "It's only right that the father of the child have a hand in the search. Go to Bridges, Camille. He's the one you should be talking to right now."

"But he's not the father."

Nicholas's tense jaw fell slack. Confusion obliterated any possibility of rational thought. "I don't understand."

"You have to help me, Nicholas." She searched his eyes, her own filled with fear and a tangle of other pained emotions. "You're the only one who can. If you won't do it for me, do it for the baby."

He shook his head. "You're not making sense."

"The baby isn't Grant's." She stared straight into Nicholas's eyes, took a deep breath. "It's yours. You're the father."

Chapter Two

Camille Wells shivered uncontrollably as she waited for Nicholas's answer. She didn't care that she had just blurted out the fact that he was a father. Or that he looked completely stunned.

Right now, she didn't care about anything but finding her baby.

He didn't look directly at her, kept his face turned slightly to the left in an effort to shield that damaged side from view. "You should sit down." The words were scarcely a whisper, wholly uncharacteristic for the gruff man he had become.

The beast. That was what the villagers called the scarred recluse who had purchased the cottage on the outskirts of town. And like the new owner, the cottage was damaged very nearly beyond repair.

With all that she knew, how could she still feel anything for him?

"I don't need to sit down," she argued. "I need to find *our* baby." Evidently the reality of what she had told him hadn't gotten through the first time. She had to make him understand.

He shook his head. "That's impossible."

Exactly the response she had expected. "We had sex, Nicholas." She drew in a deep breath, summoned her patience. Time was wasting. They needed a plan. They needed to start looking. Now! "That's how babies are made, or have you forgotten?" She trembled inside at the memory. What was wrong with her? Her baby was missing!

Another shake of his dark head. "But that was—"

"Nine months, four weeks, two days ago." Just after dark…at the same place they'd last made love. Only this time she had been the one on the verge of getting married. The irony of the situation was almost laughable. But the pain in her chest, the ache in her very soul left no room for amusement. Her baby was missing. A baby she couldn't remember giving birth to.

A baby whose first kick she couldn't recall. A baby she had carried for nine months and she had absolutely no recollection of that time save for the first four weeks. Those precious days between making love with Nicholas and walking arm in arm with her father toward her fiancé, Grant Bridges.

How could she look back on any part of that time as precious when she had cheated on the man she was to marry? They had agreed to abstain from sex the final month before their marriage to make their wedding night even more special. And what had she done?

Grant. God, he had been so good to her. He had been perfectly willing to marry her and raise the child as his own. Marrying him without telling him the truth had been out of the question. Camille had told him everything. And he'd forgiven her. Even more incredible he'd still wanted to marry her. Camille had recognized the second chance and pulled herself back together. She would be Mrs. Grant Bridges. Her child would be raised by two parents and no one would ever know the truth.

Then, in one unexpected gust of gale force wind, everything had changed.

She had lost months of her life…her baby…the future she had planned.

Everything.

"But you were going to marry Bridges," Nicholas argued as if that was a logical reason the child couldn't be his. "Did you know…?"

She nodded, shuddered at the chill that had bored deep into her bones. "I found out a few days before the wedding."

Suspicion reared its ugly head in his startlingly blue eyes. "But you were going to marry Bridges anyway."

Not a question. An accusation. She squared her shoulders. "Yes. I told him about the baby. He was willing to marry me anyway." She glared into those piercing eyes. "In fact, he insisted that it was the only right thing to do."

Her words hit the mark. She saw the sting in Nicholas's eyes. Good. He deserved it.

"When I wouldn't have," he suggested, fierce indifference pumped into his tone.

"Have you ever?" She hugged the blanket closer against the quivering she couldn't quite conquer. "Think about it, Nicholas— you never were exactly reliable. You didn't have the courage to stand up to your parents when it came to us. And then, when your grandfather died in the lighthouse fire, you deserted all of us."

Fury tightened his jaw, sent a muscle there jumping rhythmically. "I had my reasons."

That was the part that frosted her the most. "Oh, yes." She angled her head and glowered at him. "It was for my own good. For the good of all of Raven's Cliff. How could I forget?" Yet another logical excuse spawned by selfish, illogical reasoning.

"You don't understand," he snarled, that beastly side showing in his voice and in his eyes as he stared straight at her.

Camille didn't flinch. It wasn't easy. The left side of his face was disfigured from the lighthouse fire. The damage extended down his throat, along his left arm and the upper portion of that side of his torso. Camille had felt the raised, calloused skin that night they'd made love. But it hadn't been until the clouds had cleared from the moon that she'd gotten a good look at his face. The sight had stunned her, sent anguish searing through her. Her reaction had hurt him. She'd tried to explain, to apologize, but he refused to listen.

He'd pushed her away, deserted her, as surely as he had four years prior.

He hadn't given her a chance to tell him that what she really saw was the lines and angles of the handsome face he'd always had. The broad shoulders and powerful arms. The lean waist and the masculine contours of his chest.

As sorry as she was for all that he had lost, for the suffering he had endured from the burns, she would not feel sympathy for him. That soft feeling had vanished the night he made love to her and then walked away.

For a second time.

"I understand perfectly." She reeled in her emotions. They were still wasting time. What happened between them made no difference. All that mattered was finding her child. "And frankly, I don't care. I need to find my baby. Nothing else matters."

He turned his profile to her once more, concealing the left side from view. The rigid set of his shoulders and the fists his fingers had balled into told her he was considering how to handle this situation.

No matter that she had never once been able to depend on Nicholas, no matter that until his sudden so-called death he had been viewed by all of Raven's Cliff as a self-centered rich boy, Camille knew she could depend on him to help her.

Nicholas had learned something about responsibility in the past five years. At first she hadn't wanted to acknowledge it, but during the better part of the past two weeks as she had lain in that hospital room under guard, she had come to terms with many things.

She had suspected that the recluse living in the cottage was responsible for a number of anonymous gifts to the village. Everyone had talked about how some philanthropic soul had heard of Raven's Cliff's tribulations and had decided to help. But Camille had recognized a pattern. As the then mayor's daughter, she spent a lot of her time doing charitable work with her mother. On the few occasions when she had heard of the recluse's presence in town, she had begun to mentally chart what she heard about his visits along with the unexpected donations that oddly coincided with those rare appearances. Like how badly Miss Louise Patterson had needed a new playground for her day-care center. There were numerous other instances she could think of, but now wasn't the time to bring up her suspicions.

Still, those instances were solid evidence, in her opinion, that Nicholas had changed. He needed to assuage his guilt with good deeds. If playing upon that guilt was wrong, so be it.

She had to find her baby.

Anguish tore through her. "Are you going to help me?" She didn't add the "or not" that filtered through her head. He couldn't refuse her. She wouldn't let him. He could help her. She was certain. A man who had been to such dark places could no doubt reason out the thinking of someone evil enough to steal a newborn baby.

As if she'd said the last aloud, Nicholas's gaze drifted to the rough plank floors. Her heart thumped harder in her chest. *Please, please say yes.*

"What do you want me to do?"

Though he didn't look at her, his voice told her he had resigned himself to the obligation. Part of her wanted to be angry that it had taken such prodding to secure his help, but the reality was she didn't care. As long as he helped her it didn't matter why.

Another harsh reality shook her with an impact that would surely register on the Richter scale. Where did they start?

"I…" She swallowed at the lump of emotion lodged in her throat. "I don't know."

Blue eyes tangled with her own of a paler shade. Her mind immediately considered the idea that their baby would likely have blue eyes as well.

She shook her head. Absolute focus was essential. "I was found abandoned and alone." And half dead, she didn't bother adding. "No one discovered the fact that I'd recently given birth until right before I regained consciousness." The truth was the hospital staff had been so focused on keeping her alive that nothing else had mattered at first. Eventually when all other possibilities had been exhausted in an attempt to trace down the source of the near-lethal staph infection, the indications that she had recently given birth were discovered.

"Have they uncovered the cause of your amnesia?" At her questioning expression, he went on. "Raven's Cliff is a small village. I heard through my housekeeper that when you awoke you remembered nothing since falling from the cliffs."

Funny, nothing went without discussion in this small village and yet her child was missing. Someone had held her for months, delivered her baby, and then disappeared without anyone noticing. Evidently right here in Raven's Cliff.

Her legs wouldn't hold her anymore. She shuffled to the nearest chair and collapsed there. "The experts believe the amnesia is drug related. At first it was assumed that I'd suffered head trauma from the fall, but there was no indication of major or permanent damage." She closed her eyes a moment before she continued. "The theory is that I was drugged for the duration. Then, before the drugs wore off, the staph infection worsened. Between that, dehydration and God only knows what else, I slipped into a coma. My last memories are of my wedding day." She took a bolstering breath. "Then of waking up in the hospital."

The psychologist working on her case theorized that perhaps the missing time was too painful to remember. Since she was physically recovered with no apparent reason for the lapse in memory, the cause had to be psychosomatic. She couldn't rule out that theory, and quite frankly she didn't care why she couldn't remember. She only wanted to find her child.

Nicholas remained silent for an endless minute as he obviously considered all that she had told him and whatever he had heard since she was found.

"We have no way of knowing where you were held," he began, his tone somber.

Her chest tightened as she nodded her agreement.

"We have no idea who held you or why."

Another nod of concurrence wasn't necessary, and that was just as well. If she moved she might very well throw up. She couldn't even remember the last time she'd eaten, but the nagging desire to empty her stomach persisted, gained force with each passing second.

"And—" his gaze leveled fully on hers "—we don't know if the baby survived beyond birth."

Ice slid along every nerve ending, hardened in her blood. "There's no reason to think otherwise," she argued.

Was that pity in his eyes? Or regret?

"You said yourself that the experts believe you were drugged for all those months…"

He didn't have to say more.

He was right.

Maybe someone at the hospital had even mentioned that possibility to her but she had wiped it out. Denied the potential.

No. She refused to consider it now. "Lots of babies survive prolonged drug use by their mothers." Mothers hooked on illegal drugs delivered living babies all the time. There were problems, but at least the child was alive.

"My baby is alive." She dredged up her courage and exiled the fear and uncertainty.

With one downward sweep of his dark lashes, the regret or pity she'd noted vanished and was replaced by the fierce indifference of the beast. "How do you know? The odds are not in your favor. Give me one valid reason we should even bother with a search and I'll do all within my power to find your child."

Your child, not our child. Fine, if that was the way he wanted to play it.

"I only have one," Camille said, pushing to her feet so that she could look him squarely in the eyes. She swayed but steadied herself in time to prevent his reaching out to her. "I can feel it. Right here." She released the blanket, allowing it to puddle around her feet, and pressed both hands over her heart. "My baby is alive. He's out there waiting for me to bring him home."

The undamaged corner of his mouth twitched. "And you know the child is a boy."

Camille nodded. "Yes." She hadn't actually come to that conclusion until that moment, but somehow she knew with every fiber of her being that the baby was a boy. Her little boy.

He sighed, the sound weary, reluctant. "All right." He pushed the tousled hair back from his face. "We'll start with who found you. We need as much information as possible."

That would be a waste of time. "Detective Lagios has gone over what he saw that night a hundred times. He was in a car chase with the Seaside Strangler. It was dark and rainy.

The fog was thick. He almost missed seeing me lying there on the side of the road. He carried me to the clinic, and that's all there is."

"I remember." Nicholas stepped closer, bent down, picked up the blanket and draped it around her shoulders once more. "If I'm going to help you, there's one thing we must get straight right from the beginning."

He was going to help her? She shivered. His touch did that to her. It made her furious that he affected her so easily. But then, he was the father of her child.

And the only man she'd ever loved.

Don't even go there. She needed his help, nothing more. She couldn't go back down that path.

"What's that?" She fisted her fingers into the blanket and pulled it close.

"We will do this my way." He held up a hand when she would have protested. "No negotiations."

"Fine." Anything. She only cared that they got started.

"We'll start first thing in the morning."

Tomorrow? No! "We have to start now." Didn't he get it? Her baby was out there. The idea that he hadn't been fed…or bathed…tore at Camille's heart. "Right now, Nicholas. No negotiations," she reiterated, using his words.

"It's after midnight," he said quietly. "We can't storm into a person's house at this time of night and hope to achieve cooperation."

Like she had done? She hadn't considered the time. She'd come straight here as soon as she'd given her parents the slip.

"But—"

Banging on the front door made her jump. Her heart rocketed into her throat. Had her father tracked her here? He would not be happy. She hadn't told her parents who the real father was yet…she'd let them believe the child was Grant's. It was easier.

Now who was the coward?

Before she could mull over that idea, Nicholas had strode to the window next to the door and peered out past the curtain.

"It's Chief Swanson."

Goose bumps spilled across her skin. The chief thought she had hurt her baby. That she'd done the unspeakable. Had her father sent him here to bring her home?

More banging on the door jerked her from the troubling thoughts.

"Sterling, it's Chief Swanson. I need to speak with you!"

Camille didn't know what to do. Should she hide?

Nicholas held her gaze another moment. "Is there anything else I should know?" he asked.

She wasn't sure what he meant by that, but she shook her head.

He turned his attention to the door and opened it. "It's late," he said to the chief.

Swanson removed his hat and shook himself to send the water flying from his overcoat before stepping across the threshold. "This couldn't wait." His gaze landed on Camille and he blinked, clearly startled. "Miss Wells," he said with a dip of his head.

"Chief." She couldn't keep the antagonism out of that one word. How could this man, a man who had known her for most of her life, believe she'd hurt or abandoned her child?

Nicholas closed the door and folded his arms over his broad chest. "What couldn't wait?"

The chief turned his hat in his hands as if he didn't look forward to passing along whatever he'd come here to say. "Someone has leaked your identity."

The news sent a tremor of fear through Camille. Though Nicholas looked unfazed, she was certain he had to be worried as well.

"How did that happen?" he demanded. "Only you, Lagios and the village's legal counsel knew."

The chief pressed his lips together and moved his head solemnly from side to side before admitting, "I can only assume someone overheard a telephone conversation between me and Andrei." He blew out a burdened breath. "I hate to think that any of my deputies would have done such a thing, but there's just no other explanation. We both know that most folks around here, my staff included, aren't going to feel any sympathy for you."

Camille's shoulders sagged with the weight of what this meant. The citizens of Raven's Cliff would not be happy that they had again been misled by one of their own. Between her father's betrayal, Fisher's and Gibson's, the whole village was overwhelmed. One more infraction might just send any number of normally good citizens over the edge. Battle-fatigued already from a serial killer, a mad scientist and a terrorist group, anything could happen.

"I received a dozen calls in the past two hours," Swanson explained. He looked from Nicholas to Camille and back. "They're already talking about the curse."

The curse. Dear Lord. Camille closed her eyes and caught herself as she swayed again. This was too much. Nicholas needed to be focused on helping her find her child. He didn't need this insanity right now.

"I appreciate your warning me," Nicholas said, his tone resigned. "I don't care what the people of Raven's Cliff think of me. You know what I came here to do. I've waited far too long as it is."

Judging by the chief's grave expression, there was more bad news. "It's not going to be that simple, Nicholas."

Nicholas flinched at the familiarity. "What do you mean?"

"Some of them have put two and two together. They've reasoned that you've been here for the better part of the past five years. So have their troubles. That makes those who usually lend no credibility to the curse think twice." He fumbled with his hat a bit more. "They want you gone. Now. Tonight."

"No." Camille didn't realize she'd said the word aloud until both the chief and Nicholas turned to her. Her face flushed. "He…" She might as well say it. "He can't leave."

"Miss Wells," the chief said patiently, "unless he's broken a law I have no cause to run him out of town, so don't mistake what I'm here to do."

"What *are* you here to do?" Nicholas asked pointedly, drawing the chief's attention back to him.

"I'm here to warn you. It's a damned shame that some folks have to act this way, but it's only human I suppose. The fact of the matter is, I can't guarantee your safety, considering."

Considering. Fury bolted through Camille. "That's ridiculous." She took a step in the chief's direction. "When I was in the hospital, I had around-the-clock security. If you can do it for me, you can do it for Nicholas. Post a deputy outside." She thrust her hand toward the front of the cottage. "I would think you would've already taken that measure."

The chief shrugged. "I'll do all I can, Miss Wells. But the people of Raven's Cliff are pretty worked up. They've been through a lot. Some folks aren't thinking rationally."

"I appreciate your efforts," Nicholas said. "But I can handle this myself."

"I don't—" Whatever the chief would have said was interrupted by his cell phone. He pulled the phone from his belt. "Swanson."

Camille's burst of adrenaline abandoned her, leaving her weak and feeling defeated. What did they do now? Finding her child had to be priority. If anyone got in the way—

The chief's call ended and he tucked the phone back into his belt, dragging her attention to him once more. "Looks like we're about to find out just how ugly this is going to get."

The air in Camille's lungs evacuated.

"There's a riled-up mob headed this way. My deputies are trying to dissuade them, but they're not cooperating."

Before Nicholas or Camille could respond, the sound of angry shouts erupted outside.

The chief rushed to the window and looked out, then turned back to Nicholas. "They're here."

Chapter Three

Nicholas stepped back from the window. At least a dozen villagers had climbed out of the four vehicles parked haphazardly in front of his cottage. The darkness shrouded their faces and whatever weapons they carried. Two police cruisers, blue lights throbbing, had screeched to a halt in the narrow street. Judging by the angry shouts, cooperation wasn't part of the plan.

"Nicholas, you and Camille stay inside and let me and my men handle this," Swanson ordered.

Since Camille had apparently walked through the rain to get here, there was no vehicle outside to give away her presence. The last thing Nicholas wanted was for her to be dragged into what was likely to happen.

He pushed aside the news she had announced. Now was not the time to contemplate the unexpected emotions the revelation had evoked. There was an immediate decision to be made.

This could turn into a violent confrontation. Nicholas had no desire for any of the villagers, whatever their intent, to be hurt or arrested. This, all of this, was his fault.

He turned to the chief. "Obviously they have questions for me. Hiding won't change how they feel. I need to give them the answers they seek." He couldn't change the fact that more than likely all of Raven's Cliff now knew his identity. It was time to face the consequences of his secretive presence.

"Mr. Sterling," Chief Swanson argued, his tone firming into one of judicial formality, "I'm certain that's not a good idea. You just stay in here and I'll get these folks settled down. You go out there and there's no telling what might happen."

"He's right." Camille moved closer, her expression worried. "Don't go out there, Nicholas."

Nicholas didn't miss the frustrated look the

chief sent in her direction. Did this man actually believe that Camille would be capable of abandoning, giving away or somehow hurting her own child? Impossible.

"Stay with the chief," Nicholas instructed Camille.

"Sterling," the chief protested as Nicholas reached for his overcoat, "whatever score you believe you have to settle with those folks would best be settled when emotions aren't running quite so high." As if to punctuate his statement, Raven's Cliff's official representative of the law stepped in front of the door.

Chief Swanson had no idea of the score, as he called it, Nicholas had to settle. "Unless you're going to arrest me," he said bluntly, "step aside and allow me to do what I must."

"You can't go out there," Camille urged. "They've been through a lot, Nicholas," she added gently, "we all have. Let them get used to the idea that you're alive before jumping into a confrontation."

Her tawny curls were still damp. Strands clung to her soft, pale cheeks. It would be easy to take her advice, but he'd taken the easy way out for far too long as it was. It was past time to do this right.

"Keep her in here," he said to the chief. "I don't think her parents would be too happy if you allowed her to get caught up in this."

Nicholas pushed past the chief and walked out the door before further arguments could be raised. He knew what he had to do, and there was no putting it off. The truth was out now. As Camille said, the people of Raven's Cliff had been through tremendous challenges.

He wasn't going to drag this one out any longer than necessary. Careful to keep his right profile turned to the crowd, he moved a fair distance from the dim glow sifting through the rotting drapes of the cottage windows.

"That's him!" a voice shouted from the dark perimeter of the yard.

Raven's Cliff's finest had kept the mob off Nicholas's property to this point. The small crowd loitered at the roadside, the moon spotlighting their angry demeanors. Keeping them that far away couldn't have been an easy task.

Murmurs and more shouts rumbled through the crowd, most directed to one another.

"You brought back the curse!" a man

shouted as he pushed past the deputy struggling to restrain the crowd. "All of this is your fault!"

Others joined him, breaking the perimeter and daring to step onto private property. Property owned by the beast. Few of the villagers had gotten a close look at Nicholas, and he intended to keep it that way. The few who had had wasted no time in spreading the rumors of his hideous side.

At the first lull in the ranting, Nicholas spoke. "Legend would confirm your accusations," he admitted. "But living in the past won't change the future…or the present. I've returned to Raven's Cliff, my home, to rectify my mistakes."

"Considering all that's happened, you're a little late, aren't you?"

Nicholas squinted to get a better look at the man who had stepped forward. Rick Simpson. The new mayor.

"Yes." Nicholas didn't bother defending himself. He was guilty. He had failed his grandfather and all of Raven's Cliff. "I will—"

"There'll be more trouble!" a woman shouted.

Nicholas didn't recognize her but her accusation carried significant weight.

"The only way to be rid of the curse once and for all," a man who looked vaguely familiar to Nicholas offered, "is to run him out of town for good."

This was the reaction Nicholas had expected. "You don't understand—"

"You folks should be helping with this situation, not adding fuel to the fire." The chief surveyed the crowd. "Chapman, are you seriously taking part in this?"

Stuart Chapman, the owner of the general store. Nicholas had thought he recognized the man who had a reputation for always getting along and never taking sides. The mountain of a man was usually friendly... even to the beast.

"Look what he's done, Chief," Chapman argued. The crowd reiterated his assessment. "If he doesn't go, more trouble will come. Haven't we suffered enough? How many more friends and neighbors have to die before this monster is finished?"

Nicholas flinched in spite of being accustomed to being considered just that. A monster. The beast. He'd been called both names many times.

"Go home, Stuart," the chief urged, his patience clearly at an end. "Take these good folks with you. Mr. Sterling has done nothing wrong. Unless he breaks the law, he has just as much right to be here as any of you."

As if the new mayor had only just recognized the best interests of the citizens he represented, Simpson put up his hands. "Chief Swanson is right. We should all go home and ponder a way to make the best of this unpleasant situation."

The crowd wasn't easily persuaded, but after a few more shouts in Nicholas's direction and some prompting by the deputies and the mayor, the exodus finally began.

Simpson was the last to climb into a vehicle. He stared at Nicholas from across the yard as if daring him to react. He might pretend to be going along with the chief, but he obviously wasn't finished yet. Nicholas refused to rise to the bait. He would not give the bastard the satisfaction.

Nicholas had much larger problems.

"This is how it's going to be from now on,"

Swanson said wearily as the trucks and SUVs roared away. His deputies followed the caravan along the narrow, winding road that led back into Raven's Cliff proper. "You might want to consider if this is really what you want to do, Sterling."

Nicholas turned to the chief. "I know what I have to do. All I need is what is rightfully mine to start the process."

Swanson nodded. "The village attorney, Mason Cates, is working on that." The chief pushed up his cap and scratched his balding head. "We thought you were dead, Nicholas. Eventually the village had to do something with the property, but the legal kinks will be worked out and then you can take possession of your family's estate. It's just gonna take a little more time."

Blake Monroe would need to be reimbursed for the work he'd done on the manor. Nicholas would make that right once the legalities were settled. All of it was taking far too much time. Time was the one thing Nicholas didn't have. "The longer we wait," Nicholas warned, "the worse things will get." He didn't bother bringing up the curse.

The chief knew what he meant. The evil that Nicholas felt in the air was building in intensity. Soon, very soon, there would be more trouble.

And a few irate villagers would be the least of the chief's problems.

Swanson exhaled a bothered breath. "Yep, that's what I'm afraid of."

"What're you going to do about this, Chief?"

Nicholas and the chief turned at the sound of Camille's voice. She'd stepped out onto the stoop, the blanket still wrapped around her.

"The only thing I can," Swanson admitted. "Deal with whatever comes up as it happens."

"You should go home," Nicholas insisted. She had gotten soaked to the bone. Considering her recent health ordeal, walking here in the rain hadn't been a rational idea.

Camille's gaze collided with his. "You made me a promise, Nicholas. The longer we wait…"

She didn't have to say the rest. He understood what he had to do. What she desperately wanted him to do. "I'll call you in the morning. We both need a good night's rest if we're to be adequately prepared."

The chief looked from one to the other, completely puzzled. "What's going on?"

"My baby is missing," Camille snapped. "No one in your office seems to care."

"You know that's not true, Camille," Swanson argued. "We're doing all we can to find some answers."

Camille laughed, but the sound lacked any hint of amusement. "Oh, yeah. I know just how hard you're working. You think I did something wrong." The pitch of her voice got higher and the sound angrier with each word. "You're not looking any further than that." She started to shake. "While my baby is out there with some…some…" Emotion got the better of her then. Her hands went to her face and she sobbed.

Nicholas ached with the need to hold her, to comfort her. But the chief was watching, analyzing.

To hell with it. Nicholas strode to her, wrapped his arms around her and held her close. "We will find your baby. Whatever it takes."

The reality that he couldn't focus on restoring the lighthouse until he helped

Camille find her baby haunted the fringes of his mind.

But that couldn't be helped.

A child was missing.

Camille's child.

His child.

"THANK YOU, CHIEF." Camille said the words though she didn't feel the slightest bit grateful to the man.

But he had given her a ride home.

That was something.

Though the rain had stopped, a chill had permeated the air, held close to the ground by the consuming fog. She shivered as she hurried up the sidewalk to the front door of her parents' home.

She hadn't been thinking when she'd sneaked out the back door and run through the storm to find Nicholas. She'd tried to sleep, but she just kept going over and over everything the chief had said earlier tonight. She'd heard him talking to her parents when he'd stopped by to give an update. He believed Camille had suffered some sort of psychotic break during the kidnapping and that she either knew what the kidnapper had done with her child or had abandoned the child herself in order to seize the opportunity to escape her abductor. That theory had likely come from the psychologist. He hadn't laid that scenario out in a neat little line to Camille, but he'd hinted at the idea.

How could he or anyone else believe she would sacrifice her child to save herself?

She shuddered.

With only one option, she had taken it. Nicholas would help her find her child. What anyone else said or thought didn't matter. Together they would succeed.

They had to.

Camille retrieved the key from under the rock by the steps and as quietly as possible unlocked the front door. If her parents discovered she had left the house there would be trouble. Since her release from the hospital they had treated her more like a prisoner or a rebellious child than a grown woman.

When the door opened without a creak, Camille breathed a sigh of relief. Holding her breath once more, she closed and locked it. Now all she had to do was make it to her room. The same room where she'd slept until she'd gone off to college.

The house was dark and silent. Her parents were likely dead to the world, her mother with the aid of her tranquilizers while her father would have drank himself into oblivion. According to her mother, since resigning as mayor of Raven's Cliff he'd sought refuge in the bottle. For the first time in her life, Camille feared for her parents' marriage. As much as she loved her parents and as selfish as it sounded, she couldn't worry about their troubles at the moment. Finding her baby was all that mattered. Her parents were adults, they could take care of themselves.

Her baby was vulnerable and helpless.

Emotion crowded into her throat, swelled in her chest. Approximately five weeks old. That was how old her baby would be now. The gynecologist had estimated that Camille had given birth four and a half to five weeks ago.

Had she gotten to hold her baby? Her breasts were still tender. In the hospital they had given her something to make her stop lactating. Had she nursed her baby that first week or so before she'd been left to die?

As crazy as it sounded, Camille prayed that her abductor had sold her baby to some caring couple who couldn't have a child of their own. She'd read on the Internet where couples at times turned to less-than-legal means to adopt a child. The idea that her child was with a loving couple was a far better one than the possibility that he had been abandoned somewhere and left to die as Camille had been.

Anguish ripped at her insides. *Please, God, don't let my baby be dead.*

Camille felt for the light switch in her room. She needed a shower and some sleep. Nicholas was right about that. She would be able to think more clearly if she was rested. Sleep would come easier now that she knew he was going to help her.

"Where have you been?"

The oxygen trapped in Camille's lungs as she blinked against the light. Beatrice Wells sat on Camille's bed, the tight features of her face confirming the fury in her tone.

"Mother." Camille summoned her wits. "What're you doing up?"

Beatrice stood, arms crossed over her chest. "Worrying about you, what else?"

Camille had thought for certain her parents were asleep when she'd left. Well, she couldn't change the fact she'd been caught red-handed. The most she could hope for was to lessen the unpleasantness of the battle to come by playing on her mother's sympathy.

"I had to get out of the house." Camille allowed her mother to see the despair and fatigue consuming her. "I couldn't sleep."

Beatrice moved toward Camille, the pink slippers on her feet a perfect match to the flowing gown and robe. Beatrice Wells never looked less than perfect, even in the middle of the night after months of tragedy.

Her mother brushed a wisp of hair from Camille's cheek. "You shouldn't have left the house at night alone." She moved her head from side to side. "You're not well and I'm not so sure Raven's Cliff is safe anymore. Not after…all that's happened."

"Chief Swanson thinks it was the Seaside Strangler who held me for so long," Camille said, her weary mind latching on to her mother's suggestion. "His other victims were drugged." Camille had also heard that he'd attempted to use another pregnant woman in his heinous plans. "He's dead. He can't hurt me or anyone else now." But what had he done with her baby? Had the baby even been born before his death? Was he even the one who held her?

The same frightening questions bombarded Camille. She struggled to keep them at bay, to stay focused on the present. If she allowed herself to dwell on the unknown, she would lose her mind.

"Where did you go?" The suspicion was back in her mother's eyes. "Your friends surely don't keep such late hours on a work night."

Camille shrugged. "I went for a walk. No place special."

Beatrice smoothed a hand over the blanket still draped on Camille's shoulders. "Really? Where did you get the blanket? It's not one of ours." She said the last with a tone that bordered on disgust.

Trepidation nipped at Camille. She was twenty-nine years old. A college graduate, summa cum laude. She'd been financially independent for years before...all this insanity. How could her mother treat her as if she were a troubled teen? As if she were untrustworthy?

The fact was, everyone was treating her that way.

"I'm tired." Camille decided then and there that she wasn't going to play this game. She did not have to answer to her mother for her whereabouts. "I'm going to bed."

Camille stepped around her mother and let the blanket drop to the floor. She decided not to bother with the shower and just climbed into the bed. Exhaustion clawed at her. She needed to sleep. Tomorrow they would start the search.

Soon she would have her baby back.

Camille would make sure she never lost her child again. She would keep her baby boy safe. Give him everything he needed.

Except a father.

How could Camille ever hope to make Nicholas a part of their child's life? He wanted nothing to do with her. Had exiled himself from the human race. Yes, he had agreed to help her but that was probably more from the fledgling sense of compassion he possessed than any sort of feelings for her or their child.

Grant would still gladly marry her. But she

couldn't do that to him. She could never love him the way he deserved to be loved.

Camille closed her eyes. She just couldn't deal with that. She would raise her child on her own. She didn't need anyone else.

"Did you go see *him?*"

The question startled Camille. She hadn't realized her mother was still in the room.

How could she have guessed that Camille would go to Nicholas? She had to be fishing. Pulling the covers up close to her chin, Camille opened her eyes and turned toward her mother. She worked hard at keeping the surprise from her expression and her voice as she responded. "Who is *him?*"

"Don't pretend you don't know who I'm talking about." Beatrice scrutinized her daughter's face. "The hospital staff told me he came to your room every night while you were in that coma. I was appalled when I found out Chief Swanson had allowed him to sit at your bedside every single night for days."

Camille threw back the covers and sat up. "What're you talking about?" Nicholas came to the hospital? Sat by her bed every night? Why hadn't anyone told her?

"It doesn't matter." Her mother placed a hand on the light switch near the door but hesitated before leaving. She pointed a knowing look at Camille. "I know who he is. Don't be foolish, Camille. He used you once, knowing his family would never permit a marriage between you. Don't go crawling back to him now that he is nothing and needs you. Think of your pride."

Her pride? That was the last thing on her mind. "The only thing I'm thinking about right now is finding my baby." She hurled the words vehemently. Her mother flinched. "The past no longer matters. All that matters is my baby."

"Your father and I have already contacted a private investigator. He'll find the truth."

A new rush of surprise surged in Camille. "Why didn't you tell me?"

For two days Camille had begged her parents to help her find a good private investigator. Since she had been missing for all those months, her own financial resources were drained by medical expenses not covered by the insurance. She had nothing left of her own except her car and her small house. A house she hadn't even been allowed to return to. The chief insisted she remain under close supervision.

Her whole life had been stolen from her.

"We were going to tell you in the morning." Her mother tightened the sash on her robe. "As for the other, don't be foolish, Camille. You need your father's support right now. I don't think you want him to discover that you've been in touch with that…man. What would Grant think? I'm certain he's worried sick about the baby, too. You should rely on him right now, not that loathsome beast."

Guilt pricked Camille. She hadn't told her parents that the baby wasn't Grant's. She'd let them assume what they would. Grant hadn't said anything either, obviously. Just another indicator that he deserved better than she could give him.

A frown furrowed its way across Camille's brow. "How did you know?" She searched her mother's face, but saw nothing. Beatrice Wells was too good at putting on her public mask to ever allow anyone, even her own daughter, to see anything she didn't want seen. But Camille really didn't need to ask.

Her mother and Rick Simpson, the former mayoral aide turned mayor, had always been very close. The instant Rick knew, her mother knew.

"Everyone knows. It's all over the village. Ingram Jackson is Nicholas Sterling. He's been here all along. Maybe those who believe in the curse are right. The trouble began with him, and it looks as if it will end with him as well."

Before Camille could ask what that mysterious statement meant, her mother shut off the light and walked out of the room, closing the door behind her.

Camille didn't believe in curses. She believed in evil people. Nicholas Sterling might be a lot of things, but evil was not one of them. Selfish, yes. Spoiled, yes. But he had paid dearly for those self-centered traits.

He was the only man she'd ever really loved. He was the father of her child.

She curled into a ball and struggled to hold back the tears.

Please, God, please let my baby be safe... wherever he is. Even if I never get him back, let him be safe.

But she would get him back.

Nicholas had promised to help her. That was all the reassurance Camille needed.

Chapter Four

The hours crawled by until dawn.

Nicholas had paced the floor for the unending duration of each one.

The ancient floors creaked with every step. He'd inventoried the cracks in the plaster of the walls and ceilings, the places where the paint continued to peel despite his housekeeper's earnest efforts to clean every square inch.

He glanced at the clock. At seven he intended to call Chief Swanson to learn what steps were being taken in the case. Nicholas had heard the preliminaries of how Camille had been found but at the time he hadn't known there was a second victim.

An infant.

His child.

Why would God do that to a child? Give it a father like him?

Nicholas did not deserve a child. His life was plagued with a generations-old curse. Any offspring of his would suffer the same fate. He plowed his hands through his hair. If the child was a boy as Camille insisted, would he be forced to pass along the requirements his grandfather had passed on to him regarding the care of the lighthouse?

He dropped his hands to his sides in defeat. What had he done?

For five years he had thought the worst of his sins was his abandonment of his obligations where the lighthouse was concerned. But now he knew differently. He had selfishly fathered a child to inherit the same life-altering responsibility.

And until the lighthouse and lantern were restored, there was no way to know how and when the curse would strike next. Nicholas closed his eyes and tried to slow the thoughts churning in his head. Five years ago he would have laughed at himself. He hadn't believed in the curse. Considered his grandfather's stories nothing more than tales designed to keep the legend alive, to ensure the legacy of what a sad, bitter, old sea captain had started. Not that he had ever doubted his grandfather's beliefs. The man had lived and breathed his obligation to the lighthouse.

Now he understood why his grandfather's faith had been so solid.

He had been right to believe.

That night in the lighthouse five years ago, Nicholas had heard the voice of truth.

His grandfather's voice, yes. But another voice as well. A voice that had warned him that Raven Cliff's salvation lay inside him. That he, Nicholas, was the village's only hope for survival.

Eventually, when his burns had healed sufficiently, he'd come back to make right the wrong he had caused with his dereliction of duty.

At first he hadn't completely understood what was required of him. He'd attempted to make restitution by supporting the village wherever help was needed. Despite the fact that he'd been deemed dead by all who knew him, he'd been able to access his trust. The money was more than enough to support him and any purposes he chose. But his philan-thropic deeds hadn't been enough. Then the real evil had started and his quest was obscured. By the time he'd realized his true destiny his path to that end was blocked. The village council had deemed his family estate near condemnation. They had taken steps to sell the property. Blake Monroe had taken on the challenge. Nicholas could not assume control of his family estate without revealing his identity.

The lighthouse was out of his reach.

The lantern was out of his reach.

Then, when the chief had learned who Nicholas was, the property transfer had been halted. Even then Nicholas had been forced to wait. Finally it appeared he could move forward. Restoring the lantern would be the most difficult task. The special lens had been destroyed in the fire. But that difficulty had been anticipated. A second lens had been built at the time the original was designed. The ad-ditional lens had been hidden for safekeeping.

But Nicholas knew it would be on the estate somewhere. He could feel it in his gut. It was there…waiting for him to do his part.

But first he had to help Camille.

Finally the time arrived for him to visit the chief. Nicholas drew on his overcoat and lifted the hood to conceal his face. His housekeeper would not arrive for another hour but she had her own key. She would let herself in and go about her business with or without his presence.

This day Nicholas decided to walk into town. The sun was up and shining as if the heavy rains of last night had not occurred. The air was clean and crisp with the autumn chill. The walk would do him good. It would also prove to the villagers up and about at this hour that he had nothing to hide. That he was, indeed, alive and here to stay.

His quest would not be thwarted.

As he neared Raven's Cliff proper, Nicholas could already feel the weight of gazes upon him. Those attending to their ships at the docks, those preparing to open their shops, all would be watching the hooded stranger's approach.

As Nicholas reached the center of town he paused and looked around. This was his home, too. He had a right to be here. Soon these people would know that he was not here to do harm. He wanted to help.

His arrival at the village police headquarters had the usual effect. Each member of personnel stopped his or her work to glance his way, even if they tried valiantly not to. He was a regular one-man circus act.

"I'm here to see Chief Swanson," he said to the dispatcher manning the desk.

"He's in his office." The deputy waved Nicholas through as she reached for the ringing telephone.

Nicholas nodded and made his way to the chief's office. He knew the route well. He'd been there numerous times before. The last time when he was suspected as being the Seaside Strangler.

Seated behind his desk, telephone clutched between his shoulder and ear, Swanson waved Nicholas into his office. "I'll look into it," he assured the caller. "Yes, ma'am. G'bye."

Swanson looked up as he placed the phone back into its cradle. "What can I do for you this morning, Mr. Sterling? I hope you haven't encountered more trouble already?"

The chief spoke as if just any citizen of

Raven's Cliff had entered his office, but Nicholas knew that beneath that pleasant expression resided considerable dread and no small amount of dislike. Nothing Nicholas hadn't earned.

Nicholas closed the door before taking a seat. If the move surprised the chief he kept it hidden along with the rest of what he no doubt felt.

"I'd like to know what you're doing to find Miss Wells's child." Nicholas was careful not to refer to Camille too familiarly. The question itself would rouse enough suspicion.

Swanson reclined in his chair and appeared to deliberate the question. Finally, he inclined his head and searched Nicholas's eyes. "I would ask what your interest in the case might be, but since Miss Wells was at your home last night and made it clear that you were going to help her I'll assume the two of you are friends *still*."

Still. Nicholas veered away from that line of discussion. "I would like to help in any way possible. We have a history, as you well know. Helping Camille during this painful time is the least I can do." If what Camille had told him about the investigation being a sham was accurate, Nicholas doubted his help or his interest would be wanted. No matter. He had learned the hard way to weigh all options before making any decisions. Camille was acting on emotion. Nicholas needed to hear the other side of the story first. Impulsive reactions had cost him all that was dear to him.

Another lengthy pause elapsed before Swanson offered his response. "I've contacted the FBI. They will be launching their own investigation. Meanwhile, I've got two of my men looking into the case."

Which meant no one was actually out there searching. "Are you at liberty to discuss what theories you've developed at this point?" Nicholas resisted the urge to get up immediately and start looking for the child himself. An infant was missing and no one was doing anything beyond strategizing it would appear. He bit back the compulsion to say exactly that.

Swanson flared his hands. "I don't see why not. There's not that much to know. Miss Wells was discovered by one of my finest detectives, Andrei Lagios. She'd been dumped on the side of the road and was scarcely alive. The area where she was dumped was searched three times, twice by my folks and once by the state forensics team. Not a speck of evidence was found, not even a tire mark."

"Lagios doesn't believe my brother could have dumped her there?" Nicholas gritted his teeth at the thought of his demented identical twin. He was dead now so his miserable existence could no longer harm anyone. But there was no way to know all that he had done before he took that lethal plunge from the lighthouse.

Swanson shook his head. "Not unless he was hauling her around in the trunk of his car that night. But we found no trace evidence in the vehicle to indicate that Miss Wells had been a passenger. It's like she just appeared out of the mist."

But they both knew that wasn't the case.

"And the child?"

The chief shook his head. "The truth is, we're completely confounded." He hesitated a moment. "I've interviewed Grant Bridges. He insists Camille would never do anything to harm her child. According to him, she was excited about having a child." Swanson shrugged. "She evidently knew she was expecting before she disappeared. They had discussed it and decided that having a child right off the bat would be a good thing."

Nicholas's mouth tightened.

"Frankly, I don't believe Camille would purposely harm a living soul, much less her own child. But the fact of the matter is, she's here and the child isn't. It's possible, considering some of the headlines of the past, that the kidnapper discovered the pregnancy and wanted the child and not Camille. However, that doesn't explain why she was abducted in the first place since, according to her and Grant, no one else knew about the pregnancy."

"You were there," Nicholas suggested, "the day she fell?" There really was no reason to ask; the entire village had been present. Mayor Wells's popularity had still been high at the time. No one in Raven's Cliff would have missed the elaborate wedding of his daughter.

"Sure was," Swanson confirmed. "That gust of wind blew up as suddenly as an uninvited in-law at a family reunion." He leaned forward and braced his forearms on his desk. "You see, that's part of what doesn't add up. Her fall wasn't planned. It just happened. She had to have washed up on shore somewhere and got hauled off before our search parties reached her location. It's like whoever snatched her was watching for some reason and took advantage of the opportunity."

Nicholas could see his diabolical brother doing just that. "But then there was no ransom demand."

"Precisely my point," Swanson agreed. "Why go out on a limb and take advantage of an opportunity if you're not going to see it through?"

Unless you had another plan already in motion. Nicholas decided to toss his theory into the mix. "If Alex Gibson—" aka Alexander Sterling "—was the one who found her and hid her away, he may have intended to use her as leverage if the need arose. When he discovered her pregnancy he may have hoped to use the child as a sacrifice."

"He certainly intended to use Jocelyne Baker and her unborn child," Swanson noted, then cocked his head. "But then, why wait till the baby's born. He'd intended to use Ms. Baker while she was pregnant."

"If it was Alex," Nicholas surmised, "there had to be a reason he kept Camille all that time. The bigger question is, who took care of her after Alex's death?"

Swanson sat up straight. "I guess we'll never know. But we'll do what we can to solve as much of this mystery as possible."

Now Nicholas understood Camille's frustration. The lack of urgency in the chief's manner irked him.

"Meanwhile, the child could be in danger."

"The feds will do all they can to find the child," the chief argued. "After all, they have a special unit dedicated to finding missing children."

"But you aren't going to launch a search of your own?" Nicholas countered, fury knotting in his gut.

Swanson threw up his hands. "Where? We don't have the resources to take on that broad a search. I've got two men working the case. We've got APBs out. Every news channel from Portland to Bangor is running pleas for information. All we can do is react to the leads that come our way."

Before Nicholas could make the bitter comment hovering on his tongue, the chief went on, "Don't think we didn't look for that baby." He wagged a finger at Nicholas. "We searched the area where Camille was found for three days straight. We tore Gibson's room apart at the inn. We did all we knew to do and came up empty-handed."

Nicholas tamped down his irritation. The chief had tolerated a great deal more of his attitude on the subject than he'd expected. Antagonizing the man wouldn't lend itself to continued cooperation.

"I understand." Nicholas paused, watched the chief relax a fraction. "I'm not sure Miss Wells does, but then nothing short of finding the child is going to make her happy. And that's understandable."

"Of course." Swanson reclined in his chair once more. "But I imagine that baby is long gone by now. Excuse my frankness, but I'd say either it's dead or it's been sold on the black market. That kind of thing happens far more often than most folks realize."

An agony the likes of which Nicholas had not experienced before swelled inside him. The overwhelming emotion shook him. He'd been certain nothing could ever touch him the way holding his dead grandfather had, but this…*this* was almost more fierce than that clawing misery. Just like then, Nicholas was helpless to rectify the situation.

"If you have any influence with Miss Wells," Swanson offered, "you might urge her to cooperate with the feds. Let them handle this. As I said, they have the resources and the proper channels for this kind of thing. Meanwhile we'll follow every lead we get." He heaved a troubled breath. "I just don't know what else we can do."

Nicholas stood. "Thank you, Chief Swanson. I'll talk to Miss Wells."

Shouting in the corridor outside the chief's office drew Nicholas's attention toward the door.

"I don't care who he's got in there!" a male voice yelled. "I need to see the chief."

The door opened at the same instant that Nicholas recognized the voice. He tensed.

"Mayor Wells." Chief Swanson pushed to his feet.

Though Wells was no longer mayor of Raven's Cliff, old habits were hard to break, Nicholas supposed. Obviously the chief wasn't about to get on the man's bad side. Money was power, and though Wells no longer carried any political weight he still had money. Old money.

"You!" Wells jammed his finger in Nicholas's face. "Stay away from my daughter."

Nicholas should have expected this. He'd stayed clear of the family while Camille was in the hospital, visiting her only after everyone else had gone home. But her father was bound to hear about her showing up at the cottage last night.

"Now, now, Perry," Swanson said as he skirted his desk, "let's not make a public spectacle."

Outside the chief's office half a dozen members of his staff had gathered.

Wells slammed the door shut, then turned his fuming glower back on Nicholas. "You stay away from her, do you hear me?"

Nicholas wondered what the pompous man would have to say if he knew that Nicholas was the father of his grandchild. The thought gripped his chest like a vise. He would not use the child for anything, assuredly not revenge or leverage.

Swanson sidled up next to the former mayor. "Mr. Sterling was just on his way out, Perry. We can speak privately once I've seen him out."

"I want him to hear what I have to say," Wells demanded. "That's why I came here."

The ex-mayor still had spies all over the village. Otherwise he wouldn't have known Camille had been at the cottage last night. And he certainly wouldn't have known Nicholas was here now.

"Say what you have to say, Wells." Nicholas looked straight into the other man's eyes. He wasn't afraid of whatever was on Wells's mind. Ugly words and nasty sentiments were the least of Nicholas's worries just now.

"You almost ruined her life once," Wells snarled, "I won't have you destroying what she has with Grant. She deserves a life with him."

Nicholas couldn't agree more. "You're absolutely right. I have no intention of causing trouble for anyone."

"That's the thing," Wells sneered, "you are trouble. Your coming back here has nearly destroyed all of Raven's Cliff. You would be doing this village and all its citizens a great service by leaving and never returning."

If only that were the case, Nicholas would gladly go. But until he restored the lighthouse and its unique lantern, trouble would continue to befall Raven's Cliff. He was as certain of this as he was the need to draw his next breath.

The restoration had to be accomplished.

"My only wish is to set things right in Raven's Cliff," Nicholas confessed. "The lighthouse must be restored before—"

"Rubbish!" Wells screamed. "You're here for vengeance and we all know it. You're just waiting for the right moment. I'm sure you've reveled in the terrors we've suffered already."

Nicholas was wasting his time attempting to convince this man or any of the other villagers of his true quest. His energies should be saved for the work before him. He turned to the chief. "Has the city's attorney decided when I can take possession of Beacon Manor?"

The chief's face paled. Clearly this was not a subject he wanted to discuss in front of Wells.

"Over my dead body," Wells roared. He shifted that fierce attention on the chief. "If he gets his hands on that estate we'll never be rid of him."

Before the chief could concoct a response, a deputy stuck his head through the open doorway. "Chief, the fire department got a call. We're sending backup."

Nicholas held the former mayor's scalding gaze as the chief moved around Wells to reach the door. Nicholas was vaguely aware of the two men speaking quietly, but most of his attention remained on Wells. Perry Wells had at one time liked Nicholas, back when he thought his daughter would marry into the wealthiest family in Raven's Cliff. But when the Sterlings had balked, Wells had turned on Nicholas like a rabid dog. Understandable to some degree. But they had no time to rehash the past. A child was missing. Someone needed to focus on that single issue.

"Believe what you will, Wells. My plans won't change. I'm going to restore the manor and the lighthouse as soon as I help Camille find her child."

"My daughter doesn't need your help," Wells said with all the hatred he could muster. "I've hired the best private investigator in the state of Maine. He and his people will find my grandchild."

At least that was a step in the right direction. "I hope you're right," Nicholas allowed. He was glad to hear that someone was doing something active rather than waiting to react.

Wells leaned in close, putting himself nose to nose with Nicholas. "I know about Alex Gibson being your twin. Don't you see what your family has done to Raven's Cliff? You're the last of that line. You should've stayed dead."

There were a number of stones Nicholas could have thrown back at former mayor Perry Wells. The man had all but sold out to terrorists. But Wells wasn't the kind of man to view his own transgressions in the same light as he viewed those of others. Arguing would be a colossal waste of breath.

Wells made a sound that under other circumstances might have been a laugh, but his state of mind didn't allow for humor. "The way I hear it, if you stay in Raven's Cliff you may very well end up dead." He smiled faintly, but the glitter of revulsion in his eyes was all too real. "Again."

"Nicholas."

With monumental effort, Nicholas turned his attention to the chief. That Swanson referred to him by his first name meant trouble. "Yes."

"We have a situation." Red had flushed the chief's face.

Even Perry Wells stopped glaring at Nicholas long enough to look at Swanson.

"It seems that while you've been here someone has set fire to your place."

Nicholas opened his mouth, but no words came out.

Swanson cleared his throat. "Burned that old cottage clean to the ground."

Chapter Five

"Camille."

Camille tensed at the sound of her mother's voice and the knock on her bedroom door that followed. She silently chastised herself for considering her own mother the enemy, but it was difficult to think otherwise when no one, not even her mother, understood how Camille felt.

She felt alone.

Except for Nicholas.

He appeared to be the only person she could count on right now, and even that alliance was shaky at best.

Camille checked herself in the mirror, blew out a breath and went to the door. She was dressed and ready to go meet Nicholas. He'd promised they would start looking for her baby first thing this morning.

"I was just leaving," Camille informed her mother. She wasn't going to explain her intentions or ask permission. She was a grown woman, and she didn't need her parents' blessings to do whatever she chose.

Beatrice wore a broad and unexpected smile. "My dear, you have company."

"Company?" It was barely eight in the morning. Her first thought was that Nicholas had come to pick her up but that wasn't possible. Her mother definitely wouldn't be smiling.

"Come along." Her mother took her arm. "We don't want to keep him waiting."

Camille resisted. "Him who, Mother?" Camille hadn't wanted to start the day off on the wrong foot. In fact, she'd hoped to get out of the house without a confrontation at all. Clearly, that wasn't going to happen.

Beatrice's face rearranged into that I-know-what's-best-for-you expression Camille recognized all too well. "Grant, of course. Goodness, Camille, can't you try being civil? Your father and I are doing all we can to help you but you're making the task very challenging."

Grant was here. Camille closed her eyes and steadied herself. She'd avoided him since coming home from the hospital. It wasn't that she feared a confrontation. He would be kind and understanding as always. But she just wasn't up to dealing with the guilt. If she hadn't had sex with Nicholas. If she hadn't insisted on having her wedding at the lighthouse…

"Camille," Beatrice whispered, "pull yourself together. Your life is in shambles. You must recover what you can."

Stunned at her mother's harsh tone, Camille stared at her. "This isn't helping." She needed to meet Nicholas. To start the search for her baby. Didn't anyone understand?

Beatrice took a breath. "You're right. I'm sorry, dear." A smile pushed across her painted lips. "Come along. Let's talk to Grant. He may have some ideas that will help us find the baby."

The baby…not her grandchild.

Maybe Camille was being paranoid. Her mother wasn't being mean. She was worried about Camille. She was worried about the baby. Beatrice Wells had spent so many years as a politician's wife that she'd learned to put on a smile in the worst of situations. The reaction was instinctive.

Camille patted her mother's hand. "No. You're the one who's right. Grant might be able to help."

Beatrice guided her to the front parlor where Grant waited. He stood immediately.

The smile that lifted the corners of his mouth was genuine. But even that kind smile couldn't disguise the worry etched into the features of his handsome face.

"You're looking much better." He made no move to come closer.

Camille understood. Grant wasn't sure where he stood with her. When he'd visited her in the hospital she'd been less than overjoyed to see him. That, too, he'd understood. He'd known how worried she was about her baby. He seemed to be the only person who truly comprehended what she was going through. And he was the last person who would accuse her of somehow being responsible.

Why couldn't she love him the way he loved her?

Life would be so much simpler.

Camille couldn't help herself. She went to

him and hugged him close. His spicy scent was comforting, familiar. "Thank you for coming."

He drew back and studied her face, his smoky gray eyes filled with worry. "Your color's coming back." He nodded his approval. "I'm glad you're up and around."

"I'll make tea," Beatrice suggested.

Grant beamed that brilliant smile at her. "That would be wonderful."

As soon as her mother had left the room his expression fell. "Are you really all right, darling?"

Guilt pinged Camille again at the sweetness of the endearment he used. "I'm holding up."

"We're going to find your baby," he assured her. "Your father has hired the very best private investigator and I've called the agent in charge of the investigation at the Bureau's Bangor field office. He guaranteed me they would do all within their power to find the baby."

Sweet Lord. Could he be any more compassionate? "I honestly don't know what I'd do without you, Grant." She meant that. And at the same time she realized that as good as he was, as earnestly as he would pursue her happiness, Nicholas was the man she needed for this. Nicholas had been to hell and back. According to what Grant had told her, he had experienced his twin's murderous rampages. It would take a man who had suffered those kinds of trials to track down the bastard who had taken her child.

Grant gave her another quick hug. "Let's sit."

The idea that she should find Nicholas poked her. She needed to get the search under way. Her own search.

"Grant." The decision came in a rush. "I need your help."

He studied her a moment, his brow furrowed with worry. "Anything. You name it."

"Nicholas has promised to help find the baby." Camille glanced toward the door. "But Mother and Father aren't cooperating with my need to get out there and be a part of the search effort."

Grant contemplated her words for long enough to make her unsure as to whether she'd done the right thing.

"Asking Nicholas for help was a good idea." Grant lifted one shoulder in a vague shrug.

"From what I understand he senses things we normal folks don't. Perhaps if he tapped into that ability he could help us find the baby."

Us. She understood that Grant still held out hope for their relationship. Allowing him to continue to do that was wrong, she understood that, too. But she needed him. She needed as many allies as possible.

She had to find her baby at all costs.

"That's what I was thinking." Actually she hadn't thought of that at all. She'd had other reasons for calling upon Nicholas.

"Then we should go to his cottage and start immediately." Grant stood, then held out his hand. "Come on. I'll make excuses to Beatrice."

Camille smiled, really smiled, for the first time in she didn't know how long. "Thank you."

GRANT HAD INSISTED on driving since the fall morning was unusually cool even for New England. Life in Raven's Cliff carried on as if the horrors her mother had told her about hadn't happened. Camille shuddered when she thought of all that had occurred while she was away. The poison fish that had killed so many and caused incredible violence in others. Definitely the stuff nightmares were made of. Then the village had been overtaken by terrorists. Unbelievable. More like a bad movie than a nightmare. How could one village draw so much evil?

The curse.

Camille forced the thought away. She refused to believe in the curse. If she did, then she would have to admit that her baby was likely a victim of the curse as well. Real people she could fight, some unseen force she could not.

"What on earth?"

She looked up at Grant's shocked words. A smoky haze filled the sky. Red lights flashed from the two Raven's Cliff fire engines parked in front of…the cottage.

Camille's breath caught. Nicholas!

"There he is!" Grant explained, pointing through the windshield at the dark figure standing next to Chief Swanson.

Camille hadn't realized she'd said his name aloud. "Thank God."

"Good Lord," Grant exclaimed. "The

cottage burned completely to the ground. There's scarcely anything left." He braked hard and guided his car to the side of the road.

He was right. Beyond the official vehicles and the small crowd gathered she could see the heap of charred remains where the ramshackle cottage had stood.

Camille was out of the car before Grant could round the hood and open her door. She hurried to where Nicholas and the chief stood watching the firemen soak the coals of what had once been Nicholas's home.

"What happened?"

Nicholas turned in her direction. "You shouldn't have come." He spared Grant only a fleeting look.

"You appear unharmed," Grant offered, apparently not taken aback by the slight.

Nicholas didn't look at him. "I'll live."

"Good thing Martha was running a little late this morning," the chief noted.

Nicholas grunted an agreement.

Camille's knees went a little weak. What a time for this to happen. She needed Nicholas. Maybe it was selfish of her to feel that way. But she couldn't continue to be put off where the search for her baby was concerned. It felt exactly like fate was attempting to do precisely that. Maybe the curse was real. An ache wrenched her chest. She had to find her baby.

"You should've left when you had the chance!"

Camille turned sharply at the male voice that shouted the hateful remark. A throng of villagers huddled near the road. All looked angry and ready to do battle.

Chief Swanson motioned to one of his deputies, who hustled over to quiet the group.

The realization that this was no accident struck Camille with the impact of a sucker punch. "Chief, was this arson?"

The chief shot her a look that indicated just how displeased he was that she'd brought up the subject. "Can't be sure until the fire marshal has a look."

Nicholas barked out a dry laugh. "You don't need a fire marshal to tell you what happened here, Swanson. This was arson and you know it."

"Let's not be too hasty, Nicholas. The cottage was old and in disrepair. There—"

"I'd say," Grant cut in, "that this is a good time for Raven's Cliff to do the right thing and turn Beacon Manor over to its rightful owner. It's my understanding that Nicholas has already paid the back taxes in full. The city has no further legal claim to the property. Surely the attorney has cleared up that sham of a sale."

Camille wasn't sure what all that was about. Of course if property taxes weren't paid the city eventually took control. But if, as Grant said, Nicholas had paid the amount owed, he should have the right of redemption.

Nicholas stared at Grant a long moment before turning to face the chief, who looked a little rattled at the subject. "You told him?"

"Actually," Grant cut in, "Mason Cates is a friend of mine. I called him this morning after hearing the word was out that you're back."

"I'll give Mason's office a call as soon as this mess is cleared up," the chief assured him.

Grant reached into his jacket pocket. "You're busy, Chief. I'll give Mason a call. I'm sure he'll understand the urgency considering the circumstances."

Before the chief could respond, one of the firemen waved him over.

Grant stepped aside and made the call. Camille watched him nod, his black hair shining in the morning light and she found herself wondering again how one man could be so caring, particularly since he knew that Nicholas was the father of her missing child. Grant was intelligent, good-looking, and he cared.

She truly was an idiot.

"You decided to go to Bridges, I see."

Camille met Nicholas's gaze. It was impossible to read what he was thinking. Jealousy wasn't in his character, so she could rule that out. "He came by the house to see how I was doing. I told him you were going to help me and he offered to give me a ride."

Nicholas glanced at Grant, who was still on the phone. "That's very honorable of him."

The comment irked Camille. "He is the most honorable man I know." There was a time when she would not have put anyone before her father, but that had changed in the past year and a half. The stories she'd heard since regaining consciousness hadn't helped.

The sham of a sale related to Beacon Manor that Grant had spoken of was most likely related to her father's underhanded deeds while mayor of Raven's Cliff. She vaguely recalled his having mentioned ages ago what a waste it was for the estate to continue uninhabited. "Grant has proven himself time and time again."

Nicholas looked away.

She'd said that much, she might as well say the rest. "He wants to help us look for my baby."

When Nicholas didn't comment, she added, "We can use all the help we can get."

Still no answer.

"Mark my words, Sterling!"

The angry shout startled Camille from her musings. She and Nicholas looked back simultaneously. Two deputies were ushering the group of troublemakers into their vehicles.

"Next time it'll be you burning," the man shouted before the deputy could force him into the passenger seat of one of the vehicles.

"Did you recognize him?" Camille asked, certain she didn't know the man.

"I don't know his name but I recognize his

face. He moved here last spring to work on the fishing boats."

"Sounds like a troublemaker." Camille shivered as she glanced back at the smoldering remains of Nicholas's temporary home.

"He's only saying what the others want to say."

She hoped that wasn't the case. But she'd witnessed last night's ugly scene.

"Good news." Grant rejoined them, his smile wide. "Mason says you can drop by his office to sign the necessary papers and return to Beacon Manor whenever you please."

Nicholas held Grant's gaze for five, then ten seconds before speaking. "Thank you."

The next couple of minutes were riddled with tension and nothing but the sounds of the firemen doing their jobs and the murmurings of the remaining villagers. Camille wanted to scream. She hated that the cottage and whatever possessions Nicholas owned had been burned, but she needed to do something about finding her baby.

"I have an idea," Grant announced, looking from her to Nicholas and back. "Why don't we go to Beacon Manor—" he surveyed the goings-on "—where we'll have some peace and formulate a plan for finding the baby?" He said the last with such tenderness that Camille's heart hitched.

Nicholas wasn't sure why Grant Bridges had decided to play the part of Good Samaritan, but experience warned Nicholas that the other man had an agenda.

One look at the beautiful woman at his side reminded Nicholas that she was likely his motive. If so, that was good. She would be far better off if she resumed her relationship with Bridges. He could offer her everything she deserved.

"I'll bet that old hot rod of yours is still in one of the garages," Grant suggested.

Nicholas acknowledged his comment with something that sounded more like a grunt than anything else.

Grant gestured to his car. "Let's get going then. I think the chief can finish up here without us."

The smoke had burned Nicholas's lungs. The heat from the fire had reminded him of that night five years ago when the licking flames had nearly devoured him.

But he had survived. He had a quest that could not be abandoned. Not for the villagers of Raven's Cliff or anything else.

Except for Camille and her missing child.

He clenched his jaw as he settled into the backseat of Bridges's car. Nicholas would delay what he had to do in order to help her…as promised.

That the child was his flashed in front of the troubling thoughts hammering at his brain, but he pushed it aside. Emotion would only get in the way. He had to keep telling himself that the child was hers, only hers. No child would want a father like him. Not only would Camille be better off without him but the child would be as well.

Who wanted a beast for a father?

After they picked up the keys to Beacon Manor at the city attorney's office, Bridges drove the short distance to the estate. As they traveled the final stretch of road that hugged the cliffs, Nicholas's heart rate increased. He had walked the grounds numerous times since returning to Raven's Cliff, but not once had he attempted to go inside the brooding mansion.

Now he would finally stand inside his childhood home once more.

By the time the car stopped moving, the tension was nearly unbearable. Nicholas emerged from the car, his full attention on the looming structure before him. When Bridges opened Camille's door Nicholas realized he should have thought of that. He'd cared for no one but himself for so many years that his social skills were sorely lacking.

Nicholas took his time reaching the massive double-door entry, as if he hadn't waited for this moment for weeks now. Memories of his childhood here filtered through his mind. His grandfather spent far more time with him than his father. His mother had been distant. Nicholas wondered now if her distance had been motivated by guilt for having given away one of her sons. She'd obviously done the right thing, but the decision and ultimate act had surely been heart wrenching. His parents were gone now, as well. His father of a heart attack, his mother in an accident.

So much pain and misery had lived behind the massive walls. And yet, since returning to

Raven's Cliff, Nicholas had longed to take his place here once more.

It was the only way to ensure his quest was completed. Somewhere inside this house lay the answers to all the questions that kept him from completing his mission.

Nicholas positioned the key in the lock, held his breath and opened the door.

The immense door creaked as it opened. Nicholas crossed the threshold into the cavernous entry hall. The air smelled of disuse. Signs of the man who had attempted to take control of the property and renovate were scattered about. Drawings. Abandoned tools. But Nicholas paid little attention to those insignificant items.

He scanned the family paintings, the priceless works of art, sculptures and imported rugs that were works of art themselves. His family had spared no expense decorating the mansion that had been passed down for generations to those who kept the lighthouse.

A layer of dust had accumulated. Cobwebs clung to the ceilings and light fixtures. The part that bothered Nicholas the most was the silence.

The house had never been silent.

Either his mother was playing her music or his grandfather was reciting his silly tales. When his mother had played those old records she'd collected it was the only time Nicholas recalled having seen her smile.

"You'll need the power and telephone turned on," Bridges said. "A run to the grocery store and a good dusting and you'll be in business."

Nicholas didn't say anything to that. Camille had captured his attention. She hugged her shoulder bag close to her body and studied her surroundings as if she'd never been here before. It was easy to guess that she was remembering all the times they had shared here until his parents had announced that Camille Wells was not good enough for a Sterling.

What had caused his parents to take such a stand? Nicholas had been aware that his father and Camille's never really hit it off. But what was it that pushed the antagonism to that level?

Nicholas blinked. It didn't matter. That was the past. Some parts of the past could not be righted. Were actually better off left the way they were.

"So," Camille said, dragging Nicholas from his bitter ruminations. "How do we start?"

"Let's find a place to sit," Bridges suggested. He indicated the visiting parlor on the left.

Nicholas led the way. He uncovered the first chair he encountered. Bridges did the same. When the sofa was relieved of its dusty white sheet, they each took a seat.

"Do you have a plan in mind already?" Bridges asked Nicholas.

Bridges looked directly at him when he spoke. Most who encountered him worked at not looking at his damaged face. Or worse, stared at the scarred left side. Bridges did neither. He simply looked Nicholas in the eyes as he would anyone.

"Swanson has turned the investigation over to the Bureau with the exception of following up on leads coming in from the various media promptings."

Camille shot to her feet and started to pace. "I knew it. He thinks looking for my baby is a waste of time."

Grant appeared to wait for Nicholas to respond to her assertion.

"I believe he's allowing those more qualified to do what he can't," Nicholas explained. "He has no evidence, no starting place. Nothing. He can only hope to get a lead to follow from someone who knows something."

The flush of anger that colored her cheeks let Nicholas know that she indisputably did not agree with his conclusion. That was her choice. Nicholas was by no means giving the chief undue credit. This was simply his observation.

Camille shook her head. Long, pale curls bounced despite the clasp restraining them at her neck. "He isn't doing enough. I refuse to believe there's nothing we can do."

"Your father is going to offer a sizable reward," Bridges said to her.

Camille's attention shot to him. "Since when? He didn't mention this to me. He didn't seem to think it was a good idea when I brought it up."

Bridges shrugged. "Evidently he changed his mind."

"That is a step in the right direction," Nicholas said. "If there's some scumbag out there who knows what happened, chances are he can be tempted with a large enough reward."

"Exactly," Bridges agreed.

"There has to be more we can do," Camille insisted. "I can't just sit around waiting."

"Let's brainstorm," Bridges urged as he gestured to the seat she had vacated. "We can toss out ideas until we agree on something. Nicholas has apprised us of what the chief and the Bureau are doing. Your father is, as we speak, setting his steps in motion. We have a good beginning."

His words having calmed her, Camille lowered back into the chair, still clutching her purse as if she clung to a buoy in violent waters.

"Have you tried hypnosis?" Nicholas asked her. She said she couldn't remember anything since the day she fell from the cliffs until she regained consciousness in the hospital. The entire period was a murky darkness. If the head injuries she sustained in the fall weren't responsible for her amnesia, perhaps hypnosis could cut through the haze left by the drugs, assuming that drugs were truly involved.

Camille chewed her bottom lip a moment before answering. "I wanted to try, but Mother was terrified that my condition was too fragile." Her gaze connected fully with Nicholas's. "I would like to try. It might work."

"Let me contact a friend in Portland," Bridges offered. "If there's a decent psychiatrist within a hundred miles of us, he'll know."

"That'll take time," Camille protested. "Isn't there someone in Bangor who I could see?"

"I'll call right now." Bridges reached for his phone but a distinct ring slowed him.

Camille jumped. "Oh. That's me." She dug into her purse and retrieved her cell.

Bridges walked to the window to make his call.

Camille frowned at the display before opening the phone. "Hello."

She listened briefly, then turned a stunned face in Nicholas's direction. She held out the phone. "It's for you."

Nicholas stared at the phone in her hand. Why would anyone call him on Camille's cell phone? He reached out, took the phone from her and placed it against his good ear.

"Hello."

"Nicholas Sterling?"

It was not a voice Nicholas recognized.

"Yes."

"You have a very important task before you, Nicholas Sterling."

A frown nagged at Nicholas's brow. "Who is this?" The voice was distorted, impossible to identify, but sounded male.

"That is unimportant at the moment, Mr. Sterling."

"Identify yourself," Nicholas demanded, "or this conversation is over."

Bridges turned to see what the fuss was all about, his own phone still tucked against his ear.

"You are in no position to make demands, Sterling," the voice argued. "You will listen and you will do exactly as I say or your sweet Camille will never see her child again."

Ice clogged Nicholas's veins. He moistened his dry lips and forced his throat to open. "I'm listening."

"You will not call the police. If you do, the deal is off. I will disappear and the infant will disappear with me. You will find the second lens. You will do this within forty-eight hours. If you do not, the infant will be lost forever and sweet Camille will die a slow, painful death."

Fear snaked its way around Nicholas's chest. "You assume I can accomplish what you've asked with such limiting time constraints." He glanced at Bridges, uncertain he wanted the man to know of what they spoke.

"That is up to you, Mr. Sterling," the voice said. "Fail and the child is lost. Camille will die. Do you want to be responsible for yet more tragedy?"

The dead air told Nicholas the call had ended.

He stared at the phone.

Forty-eight hours.

That noose of fear tightened, cutting off his airway.

"Who was that?" Camille asked, her voice shaking.

Nicholas allowed his gaze to settle on hers. "The man who has your child."

Chapter Six

Camille stared at the phone in Nicholas's hand as he extended it toward her.

Her baby was alive.

Her heart jolted. She had known her child was not dead. No matter what the doctors and the chief had suggested, she had felt that truth in the deepest recesses of her soul.

Grant nodded to Nicholas and took the phone from his outstretched hand. He stared at the screen as he pressed the necessary buttons to view the most recent call. "Unknown number. Damn it."

"We should call Chief Swanson," Camille urged, her thoughts whirling. "He'll need to inform the FBI. They'll need to set up a trace in case he calls again. And…"

Nicholas said nothing but his grave expression spoke volumes.

Camille searched his face, his eyes. "What is it you're not telling me?"

There was more. With the same ferocity that she sensed her baby was alive, she knew there was more. Conditions. Not mere money. Were the ransom demand a simple request for money, Nicholas's eyes would not reflect such certain doom. Anguish tore at her insides. What did this animal want?

"Does he want money?" Grant demanded, his own desperation showing. "We can meet his demand, I'm sure of it. How much does he want?"

Unblinking, Nicholas held Camille's gaze, didn't spare Grant so much as a single glance. "We can't call the police. If we do, the bargain he offered is off and we'll never hear from him again."

"Tell me," Grant reiterated. "How much does he want?"

Nicholas shifted his attention to Grant. "He's not interested in money."

Grant waved his hands as if to erase the confusing statement. "That doesn't make sense. If not money, what? What could he possibly want besides money?"

His expression hard, Nicholas shifted that piercing blue gaze in Grant's direction. "He wants something only I can give him."

Utter silence filled the immense room for three frantic beats of Camille's heart. Still no one spoke. She couldn't take not knowing. "What is it he wants from you, Nicholas? I have a right to know."

When Nicholas hesitated, her patience vanished. "Tell me!" A volatile mix of hope and worry roiled in her stomach. "Whatever it is, you have to do it. Please tell me you'll do it."

As soon as she said the words it occurred to her that Nicholas's life might be the price demanded. The bottom fell out of her agitated stomach. How could she ask him to give his own life for her child's?

His child's?

She would trade herself in an instant. But this was Nicholas. There was no reason for him to be that invested or that selfless. Not once in his life had he ever shorted himself to help another. Yes, since returning to Raven's Cliff he had given much, but none of that had left him destitute. He had given from his abundance, not his need.

Nicholas glanced at Grant again. "This is a private matter—"

"We're talking about my baby," Camille argued, anger flaring. "You can't—"

"I will," Nicholas said, cutting her off, "attempt to meet his demand. You have my word. But be aware that his request may be impossible to fulfill by me or anyone else. He's given me only forty-eight hours."

Forty-eight hours. Dear God. Was that enough time? Camille's knees tried to give way, but she fought the dizzying sensations. She had to be strong. Her baby was depending on her.

"You're talking in riddles, Sterling," Grant protested, his own lack of patience showing. "What does he want? As Camille said, she has a right to know, and though I may not, I want to help." He squared his shoulders. "I demand to be a part of this."

Camille held her breath. They only had forty-eight hours. The possibility that she should call Chief Swanson swam through her head. But the caller had warned Nicholas not to go to the police. Yet the urge to do something—anything—was very nearly overwhelming.

"Sterling," Grant urged, "you're going to have to trust us." While Camille gathered her wits, Grant took the bull by the horns. "I know you have no reason to trust anyone in Raven's Cliff. As much as you may feel you let everyone down, I'm certain you feel we've all betrayed you on some level. You mustn't allow those feelings to get in the way of what had to be done."

"You have no idea how I feel," Nicholas growled.

Grant released a heavy breath. "You're right. I can't imagine how you feel any more than I can imagine how Camille feels right now. But I want to help." He turned his palms upward in a blatant plea. "Let me help you both."

One second, two, then five elapsed with Camille still unable to breathe…then Nicholas spoke.

"He wants the lens."

The air rushed into Camille's chest. Lens? What on earth was Nicholas talking about?

"Does this have something to do with the

lighthouse?" Grant appeared as confused as Camille.

Nicholas gave a single, firm nod. "The lantern housed a one-of-a-kind lens."

Grant shook his head, his confusion, like Camille's, deepening. "But the lantern was destroyed." He frowned. "At least the parts that were glass. Didn't that include the lens?"

"Yes."

Panic seized Camille. "Then how can you give him what he wants? It was destroyed! Nicholas, you're not making sense."

Grant reached out to her, placed a comforting hand on her shoulder. "We have to stay calm, otherwise we'll never figure this out."

She tried. Really she did. But they were discussing how to bargain for her child. Her baby! God, how was she supposed to go through this without feeling panicked and desperate and a dozen other emotions?

Nicholas looked from where Grant's hand still rested on her shoulder to her. "When the lens was crafted, a second lens was prepared as a replacement in the event the first was ever destroyed. According to my grandfather it was the only way to be certain the two would be exactly the same. Identical."

Grant planted his hands on his hips and started to pace. "What's so important about this lens? It's just glass, right?" He stalled and turned to face Nicholas. "Why would anyone, other than a lighthouse keeper, have any use for it? And frankly, that technology went out decades ago."

Realization dawned on Camille. She lifted her hand for Grant to wait. "Does this have something to do with the so-called curse?" When would the insanity revolving around that stupid curse end? She, for one, had had enough. The person who took her baby was real, a human. This had to be about greed or revenge, not some stupid curse.

To her surprise, Nicholas nodded once more. "The lens was not constructed of glass. Rare gems were used to assemble the lens. The precious stones not only allowed the light focused on them to pass through but they somehow magnified the light, creating a powerful beam that could be seen for miles out to sea. It was unlike any other lens known to man."

"Like a laser," Grant offered.

"Exactly." Nicholas's expression turned distant as if he were looking back into the past. "The stones were extremely rare. Legend has it that in addition to their incredible light-reflecting quality, the stones possessed some sort of mystical healing power."

Grant's face took on a knowing expression. "In other words the stones are priceless."

"And dangerous. If," Nicholas qualified, "the legend is to be believed. In the wrong hands they could be used for evil rather than good."

Crazy. The whole story was like a bad fairy tale. "Clearly this man believes it," Camille heard herself say. Every ounce of strength and determination had seeped from her body. Unless Nicholas knew where the second lens was hidden, her baby was lost to her.

The impact of that undeniable fact had her knees ready to buckle. As if he sensed as much, Grant's grip tightened on her. Nicholas noticed. That he paid such close attention to the interaction between her and Grant puzzled Camille. Like everything else in her life just now, that strange behavior had no relevance. All that mattered was finding her baby. She moved away from Grant's touch. She didn't want to be touched right now. She didn't want to be looked at. She wanted to find her baby.

"The lens and its twin were built how long ago?" Grant asked, his full attention seemingly on the insurmountable task before them.

Camille should be ashamed of herself for overreacting to his touch. He was trying to help when he had every right to disassociate himself from her and her problems. She had to pull herself together.

"More than two hundred years ago." Nicholas threaded the fingers of both hands through his hair, his own frustration visible.

Grant rubbed at his chin thoughtfully. "How are you supposed to know where it's hidden? Was the location of the hiding place passed down through the generations of lighthouse keepers?"

Nicholas dropped his arms to his sides. "In a manner of speaking."

They were wasting time. Again. Didn't either of them understand? "You must have been given a location or some sort of map. What was the point of building a second lens if it couldn't be found when it was needed?" This was pointless. Could the Bureau use her cell phone to track down where the call had come from? She should call Swanson and tell him what happened.

Before Nicholas could answer her question, Grant asked, "How can we help? You must have some idea of where to start looking. We can work together as a team."

"First off," Nicholas said, his tone unyielding as he looked from one to the other, "there is no map. I was never given a location. My grandfather told me that the lighthouse's salvation lay with me." Nicholas crossed the room and stared out the window at the monument of which he spoke with what sounded like a combination of fear and reverence. "I didn't really understand what he meant until that night."

Nicholas wasn't sure how much he should say in front of Grant Bridges. Although there had been a time when he and Bridges were friends, he was not originally from Raven's Cliff. He had not grown up in the shadow of the lighthouse with the legend hovering so very close. As committed as he sounded, a mere transplant could never fully understand. Camille had lived in Raven's Cliff her whole life and she still had doubts.

In truth, Nicholas wasn't sure he could trust anyone with any of this…but he had little choice. As much as he wanted to, he understood that he couldn't do this alone given the time constraints. The one thing he knew with complete certainty was that he couldn't risk the child's safety by failing to do whatever had to be done.

Which meant he had to trust Bridges.

"The night of the fire," Camille prodded, drawing Nicholas back to where he'd left off. Her voice was too soft. The strain was getting to her. With all of his being he wished he could promise her a happy ending. But life rarely provided such an ending. If he was extremely lucky, perhaps he could turn this around.

"Yes. It was the night of the fire that I understood what I had scoffed at my entire life."

Bridges joined him at the window. "What was it you came to understand?"

"There was a prayer he recited to me every night for as far back as I can remember." Nicholas still wasn't sure what the foolish lines meant, but they were all he had. "His own version of an old bedtime prayer. Now I lay me down to sleep. I pray the hollows my soul to keep." That was pretty much the extent of it. There were a couple other lines, but those were nothing more than a repeat of the first two.

Camille came closer. She didn't make a sound but he sensed her approach. "Does that mean something specific to you?"

He wished it meant more than it did. "He referred to the caves along the cliffs as the hollows. He insisted that both the cliffs and the caves were safe as long as they were respected. As a child I played in and around both. My parents constantly warned me that it was too dangerous to play anywhere but in the house or the yard close by. My grandfather always winked and smiled, giving me his unspoken permission to disobey." Nicholas shook off the haunting memories. "The hollows, as he called them, were my favorite places to play."

"But," Camille began, the uncertainty in that one word ripping at his determination, "there are at least a dozen caves on those cliffs."

Nicholas couldn't bear to look at her. She was terrified that he would fail. "At least."

"Some go for miles," Bridges commented. He sounded as alarmed as Camille.

"And many intersect with others," Nicholas agreed, not bothering to sugarcoat the reality. "It's like a maze down there."

"Well." Bridges looked out at the cliffs beyond the lighthouse. "We won't accomplish anything standing here discussing the difficulties. I suggest we gather the supplies we'll need and get started."

Like a frightened animal on the verge of bolting from a predator, Camille backed away from both of them. "I appreciate that you're forming a plan, but what if your assumptions are wrong? What if we waste all that time and we don't find the lens?"

Nicholas faced her, absorbed the agonizing impact of seeing her so tortured. "I'm as certain as I can be of where we should begin."

"It's a starting place," Bridges reminded her. "And we have to start somewhere."

Camille lifted her chin as if defying her own emotions but her quivering lips gave away her losing battle. "I see your point.

Doing something is better than doing nothing. I'm…" She squeezed her eyes shut and drew in a deep, bolstering breath before meeting first Nicholas's then Bridges's eyes. "I'm just thankful for your help."

"We'll need your help as well." Bridges pointed to her purse. "Do you have a pen and paper in there?"

She nodded jerkily.

"Good. On our way into the village you make a list of what we'll need. We'll gear up and get started."

The other man's unwearied smile prompted Nicholas to turn away. He wished he had a good feeling about this, but he didn't.

All the same, as Camille had said, doing something was better than doing nothing.

OUTSIDE THE GENERAL store Camille handed Grant the list she'd compiled. "That's everything."

He accepted the list, glanced it over then opened the car door. "I'll be right back."

As much as she hated to admit it, she was glad Nicholas made no move to get out as Grant strode away from the car. Since the closest shopping was twenty miles away, she'd never walked into Mr. Chapman's store and found it empty of patrons. Risking another confrontation wasn't on her agenda. She already felt stressed to the max. More trouble would push her closer to that edge that threatened her composure and would only delay their getting down to business.

"You should go with Bridges."

Nicholas's suggestion startled her. "I thought it would be better if I stayed in the car." If she went inside there would be greetings, hugs and questions, slowing their departure. She didn't want to do anything that kept them a minute longer.

"Anyone walking past who sees you will stop to chat."

Camille surveyed the street. Shoppers and those on their way to work strolled along the sidewalks, chatting and waving to each other. He was right. If any of those people spotted her, a crowd would gather. That she was in the car with Nicholas Sterling, the beast, would only raise questions she couldn't answer.

And the news would travel at warp speed to her parents.

"Okay." She opened the door and scrambled out. A firm boost from her hip sent the door closing. She hurried around the hood of the car and across the sidewalk.

Camille didn't breathe easy until she was through the store's entrance. She dared to glance back at the car and no one seemed to have noticed the passenger still seated in the back.

"Thank God," she muttered. A quick survey around the store and she spotted Grant in the last aisle.

Ducking behind a cluster of patrons in deep debate over the coming presidential election, she managed to reach Grant without notice. He'd already picked out a couple of heavy-duty flashlights and extra batteries along with a small battery-operated lantern. Those caves would be dark as pitch.

"Finding everything?" She peeked into the basket he carried and noted the wool caps and gloves. Life in Maine ensured that even the smallest of general stores carried certain essentials. Maine weather could turn brutal rather quickly.

"Just about."

He'd also selected a box of sidewalk chalk. She picked up the box and managed a smile. "In case we get bored?" Memories of her and her older sister playing hopscotch on the sidewalk in front of the mayor's office eased some of the pressure on her chest. Camille's life had been so insane since she'd regained consciousness that she'd scarcely even thought of Corrine. She really missed her sister right now. Corrine had chosen a career serving her country. For the past year she had been stationed in Iraq. She hadn't been able to rush home while Camille was missing but she would be home next month. Camille prayed she would be able to introduce her sister to her new nephew.

The baby was a boy. Camille was absolutely certain.

"That," Grant said, dragging her from happier thoughts, "is to keep track of where we've been."

Camille got it. "Good idea." She placed the box of chalk back in the basket. "Thank you for being so supportive. And so smart." She would never have thought of marking the cave walls.

Grant smiled down at her. "There is no need for a thank-you, Camille. I would never let you do this alone. You mean the world to me. The baby, too."

Her smile faltered. Such a good man. She didn't deserve him. More important, why couldn't she love him?

The image of Nicholas waiting in the shadows, watching as she'd walked along the rocks that night a year ago, sent heat searing through her body.

Stop, she ordered the part of her who wanted to romanticize their unpleasant past. She could never be vulnerable to him like that again. She needed him right now, otherwise she would have nothing to do with him. Metaphorically speaking, she had been burned by his past as well.

She refused to contemplate how she would handle the "father" question when her son was old enough. No need to borrow trouble, she had enough on her hands as it was.

When Grant reached for a deadly looking knife and accompanying sheath she was jarred from her musings once more. "That looks ominous."

He pulled the knife free of its sheath and admired the blade. "After being plagued by poisonous fish and threatened by terrorists and a serial killer, I'd say a little protection is in order while venturing into those caves."

She couldn't argue that, but the idea still made her shudder.

Grant touched her cheek. She barely restrained a flinch. "We have no idea who we're dealing with. We have to be careful."

As usual, Grant was the voice of reason.

"What in blazes is going on out there?"

Stuart Chapman's startled question jerked Camille's attention to the store owner behind the counter. Mr. Chapman's gaze was glued to one of the broad storefront windows.

Camille found herself at the counter staring in that same direction before she'd realized she had moved. Grant was right on her heels.

Mr. Chapman reached for the cordless phone next to the cash register. "Looks like a call to the chief is in order." He handed the phone to his wife, who manned the store alongside him every day that it was open.

"Excuse me, Camille." Chapman scooted

by her, pausing long enough to add, "Good to see you out and about, missy."

"It sure is," his wife seconded even as she entered the number into the phone. "We were really worried about you there for a while."

Camille should have responded, but some innate instinct had the hair on the back of her neck standing on end and her feet were keeping her close behind the big, burly shopkeeper.

The bell above the door jingled as Chapman yanked it open. The heated voices outside streamed into the store on the crisp morning air.

"Get out of the car, Sterling!" a voice demanded.

"Yeah, be a man, you coward!" another taunted.

"Maybe he can't," someone else jeered. "He's more beast now than man."

A crowd of at least a dozen had closed in on Grant's parked car.

"What's going on there?" Chief Swanson bellowed as he crossed the street.

Camille snapped into action. She hurried around Mr. Chapman and toward the angry jerks surrounding the parked car.

"Stop!" she yelled, her anger mounting at the idea of how heartless these people—people she knew—could be. Hadn't they said enough? They had burned down his home, for God's sake.

But she was too late. As she watched in horror, the rear passenger door of the car opened and Nicholas Sterling climbed out to face his accusers.

Chapter Seven

Nicholas emerged from the car and closed the door. The thud resonated in the silence that accompanied his movements. He looked from face to face; some he recognized, some he did not.

"You have something you want to say?" he asked of the crowd. They were here to talk to him, so he might as well make himself available.

Someone, quite possibly one among this crowd, had burned his cottage to the ground. Though he had felt no sentimental attachment to the decrepit structure, it had belonged to him.

He supposed to their way of thinking, the bold maneuver had been necessary to make their point. They didn't want him here. But he wasn't going anywhere. If they were smart they would get used to the idea without pushing him further. Even he, in all his muck of guilt, had his breaking point.

"Mayor Simpson, I'm hoping you're here to help," Swanson said.

The chief of police strode up to the mayor. Simpson was one of the few Nicholas recognized. He had seen him last night in the crowd that had stormed the cottage.

"The same as you, Chief," Simpson tossed back as he adjusted his hand-tailored suit jacket. "Just thought I'd see what all the fuss was about."

Nicholas would have laughed but the circumstances were no laughing matter. Men like Simpson got away with their underhanded deeds more often than not. No doubt Simpson would be following in his esteemed mentor's footsteps.

"Did you have something you wanted to ask me, Simpson?" Nicholas inquired, shifting his full attention to the polished coward.

Simpson's startled gaze connected with Nicholas's. "I beg your pardon? I'm here in support of the citizens of Raven's Cliff, Mr. Sterling."

"I think we've seen enough trouble for a good long while to come," the chief said to the crowd at large. "We need to let the past heal. You folks should go on about your business and let Mr. Sterling be. He's broken no law. I'd sure hate to see any of you wearing these cuffs hanging on my utility belt. We're already considering suspects in a case of arson." Swanson propped his hands on his hips. "If Mr. Sterling decides to offer a reward, I sure hope whoever is responsible for last night's fire understands that arson is a federal offense."

The disgruntled group stared at the chief but made no comments to his warnings and made no move to disperse as he'd ordered.

Nicholas turned all the way around, met each hate-filled gaze that dared to let him. There was something these people needed to understand. "I'm here to stay. I thought I'd made that clear already. If you have a problem with my presence in Raven's Cliff, now's the time to speak up. Only a coward makes his feelings known in secret. Who's the coward now?"

Outrage broke out amid the throng. They

hurled more threats at him and stared at his damaged face.

Nicholas continued to look from one to the other. Let them have their fill of staring at his hideous scars. He would not back down.

"We don't want you here." One of the men, a fisherman Nicholas had seen on the docks during one of his rare trips into town, stepped forward. The same one he'd noticed in the crowds at his cottage. "You brought the curse back to Raven's Cliff with you. The trouble started with you."

"And it will end with me," Nicholas promised.

"That's enough, Albert." Swanson stepped forward when the man would have gone nose to nose with Nicholas.

"Think what you will," Nicholas continued despite the chief's obvious desire to break up the party. "Your opinion won't change the fact that I have as much right to be here as any of you." He scanned the group one last time. "So get used to it."

When the fisherman and one of his cronies made a dive for Nicholas, the chief grabbed the one nearest him. A fist collided with

Nicholas's damaged jaw. He grunted, raised an arm to prevent the next blow. Somewhere in the background he heard Camille scream.

Nicholas shoved at the man's chest, determined not to resort to violence. Another punch landed in his gut. He bent forward, grabbed for the man's fist when he reared it back a third time.

The weight pressing into Nicholas abruptly lightened. He pulled away from his attacker in time to see Grant Bridges throwing the idiot to the ground.

"You heard the chief," Bridges roared, "go on about your business and leave this man alone." Bridges glared at the crowd and executed a scissoring action with his hands. "This is over!"

"Are you all right?" Camille was suddenly next to Nicholas. She studied his face, her hands working quickly to tidy his shirt while checking him for injury.

Nicholas looked away from her. She shouldn't be attending to him in front of these people. Her kindness would only come back to haunt her. And he couldn't bear to have her touch him that way.

The thought had no sooner formed than Simpson strolled toward Camille. "I doubt that your parents will be too happy to hear you're cavorting with this animal. You've barely left your deathbed."

Camille spun around and slapped Simpson square on the jaw. "Go to hell, Rick."

A collective gasp sounded as folks stopped and stared. Camille's family had a long history with Simpson. Still, he was the mayor. No doubt rumors that she was unstable would be confirmed by her public display of violence.

"Whoa." Bridges sidled between Camille and Simpson before Nicholas could recover from his shock and intervene. "I think we're ready to go now."

Nicholas sagged against the car, his emotions abruptly overwhelming him.

"I don't want to see a scene like this again," the chief called after the scattering group. He exhaled a weary breath and turned to Nicholas. "I swear, some folks just don't know when to stop beating a dead horse."

Nicholas acknowledged his comment with a nod, opened the car door and dropped into the backseat. He had no desire to talk. He wanted out of here. Back to the only place he'd ever felt he belonged.

The caves beneath Beacon Manor.

CAMILLE WAS GRATEFUL she'd worn her sneakers and jeans. The hike down to the first set of caves was nothing less than treacherous. If Grant asked her once more if she was okay she might just slap him.

She couldn't believe she'd slapped Rick Simpson. She didn't care that he was the new mayor, but her mother was going to be mortified and seriously cross with her obviously unbalanced daughter. Camille doubted she would ever hear the end of it.

Dread was already welling at the idea of what she would face tonight when she went back home. Whatever her parents threw her way she would simply have to endure. This was too important. No matter how many fancy private investigators her parents hired, she had to do this. There were things they didn't know. She wasn't sure they needed to. Admittedly, the thought that she should tell the chief had crossed her mind again once the trouble had settled down in town.

But she'd stayed quiet.

"Careful here," Grant said as he moved down the final leg of the trail.

"I'm fine, Grant," she snapped.

Camille immediately hated that she had bitten his head off. He was only trying to help and she understood that. She had no right taking out her frustration on him.

Grant held up his hands in surrender. "Sorry."

"This way," Nicholas said above the crash of water on the nearby rocks.

The light mist of salty water felt refreshing to Camille. As a child she had loved these cliffs and the frothy water pounding the rocks. Even now being here cleansed her soul on some level, allowed her to feel the hope she'd dared not permit.

The refreshing smell of the ocean gave way to a mustier odor as they entered the mouth of the first cave. Nicholas had said this was the largest and it intersected with a number of smaller passageways that tunneled beneath the mountain below Beacon Manor.

Camille slipped twice before she found her

balance on the cave's slippery, moss-swathed rock floor.

Grant passed her a flashlight. Leading the way, Nicholas had the lantern.

"Hold up, Sterling," Grant said as he pulled out a piece of the chalk he'd purchased and marked the wall of the cave. He drew an arrow pointing in the direction they intended to go and then he put a number 1 in a circle to indicate the order of their search.

"Okay," he said, "let's get moving."

He gestured for Camille to precede him. Bearing in mind how dark and dank the cave was, she had no problem with having him protecting her back.

"Not exactly as cool as it was when I was twelve," she mentioned with a tight laugh. A part of her wanted to curl up and cry at the prospect that this could turn out to be a dead end. The stronger, more determined side recognized that it was a start. She had to believe that Nicholas wouldn't lead her on a wild goose chase. Whether he said so or not, his instincts were surely guiding him.

"That's a fact," Grant confirmed. "Things

we loved as kids are always far less fun as adults."

The pathetic attempt at conversation expired as they wandered deeper into the passageway. Nicholas moved steadily forward, his lantern like a distant beacon in the consuming darkness. Slow, steady drops of water splashing onto the rocks and into tiny puddles along the cave floor accompanied their progress. Time after time her feet slipped despite the usually reliable grip of her sneaker tread. She gasped once or twice but suppressed the response as often as possible to keep Grant from hovering so close.

In the continued silence she had a chance to think about the baby. Would her little boy have tawny curls like her own or the dark silky hair of his father? Since both she and Nicholas had blue eyes that was pretty much a given, she supposed.

Names. God, she hadn't even had time to think about names. She'd barely gotten over the shock of learning she was pregnant when she went over that ledge and into oblivion.

Maybe it was silly of her to be so convinced that her baby was a boy. But she knew.

Somehow she just knew. There was always the chance her instinct was an actual memory that still eluded her like so many others.

Nigel. Camille smiled. Her maternal grandfather had been named Nigel. Nigel it would be. She had no intention of asking Nicholas if he had a preference. She was making the decisions where this baby was concerned. Once her baby was back with her where he belonged Camille intended to restart her life. No interference would be permitted. Not from her parents, not from Grant and certainly not from Nicholas, though she didn't actually anticipate him giving her any trouble. More likely he would be glad to be rid of her once and for all. He'd made that pretty clear.

Feeling good about her decision, she promised herself that she wouldn't fail.

Camille stalled. Stared into the darkness. She'd certainly done a bang-up job so far. Her baby was missing and she couldn't even remember giving birth to him.

Would her memory return eventually?

Or maybe she could try the hypnosis.

Anything that might help would be worth

whatever she had to go through to make it happen.

"Camille?"

She jumped. "Sorry." She'd stopped moving forward. Nicholas was several yards ahead. She had to focus. There was no time for planning a future. The hours were rushing by too fast already.

Hurrying wasn't something she dared to do, but she did speed up her pace a bit in an effort to try to catch up. Didn't work. When the glow from Nicholas's lantern disappeared from sight, she hesitated.

"Where did he go?"

"Sterling!" Grant moved around her. "I'll lead until we get up to him."

"I'm here."

Camille looked past Grant. Nicholas held the lantern in front of him and waited for them to catch up.

"The passage cuts to the right here," he explained as they neared his position.

That explained why he'd abruptly disappeared from sight.

"Is this leading somewhere specific?" Grant asked.

Camille was sure she heard a hint of impatience in his tone. Was he growing frustrated at the idea that their journey appeared to be taking them nowhere or was he weary of looking after Camille? After all, she'd given him no reason to remain involved in her life. Was he doing so out of some misplaced feeling of responsibility? She would need to talk to him about that. He owed her nothing. If anything, she owed him for sticking by her when it would have been far easier to walk away.

"There's a room this way I want to check out." Nicholas turned back to the passage where it veered to the right. "You'll see."

Camille's pulse reacted to the idea that Nicholas appeared to be anticipating reaching this room. Had he played there as a boy and now recalled some clue that might help in their search?

Please, please let him locate the clues he needs to find the lens.

Several more minutes elapsed before they reached the large opening he called a room. The rock ceiling overhead soared out of sight.

"Wow." She breathed the word. The room was enormous and chillier than the tunnel had been. She shivered, wished she had worn more than her light jacket.

"Let's start with the perimeter," Nicholas directed. "We'll move around the room ensuring we cover the entire expanse of wall for as high as you can see with the minimal lighting we have."

"What're we looking for?" Camille roved her flashlight's beam over the section of wall nearest her. The same jagged rocks—some areas were smoother, some seeped water.

"Any markings or niches where items could be concealed," Nicholas explained. "Basically anything out of the ordinary."

Which meant anything that wasn't rock, water or moss. With painstaking slowness Camille began with the left side of the room. Grant took the right and Nicholas visually scoured the floor.

Each time she encountered a crack or scar in the rocky face, anticipation zinged her. But none turned out to be relevant. The work of nature and time.

As she neared the far side and Grant's somewhat faster progress, her hopes fell. The idea of how long this one room was taking and all the other passages and possible rooms started to shake her fortitude.

"Sterling!"

Camille's gaze shot to Grant. Had he found something?

She wished she had a piece of that chalk Grant had brought along. If she did she could mark her place and run over to see what Grant had found. Since she didn't and couldn't, she continued with her study of the seemingly endless wall. If anything was missed she didn't want it to be her fault.

She could hear Grant and Nicholas discussing whatever he had found but she couldn't quite piece together the implications of the snatches of discussion. Sound was distorted, not exactly an echo but elongated and muffled even more so than in the tunnel.

"Camille!"

She'd almost reached their location when Nicholas called her name.

With a quick check of the floor to look for a marker to recall her position, she hurried to where the two were crouched together. Her heart rate increased with every step.

"You found something?"

"There's a niche here," Nicholas explained. "I think it's another smaller room. I remember hiding in there as a child. But I can't fit through the opening now."

"I don't think this is a good idea," Grant argued.

"Don't be ridiculous." Camille dropped into a crouch next to him and directed the beam of her light into the narrow opening. "I'll be fine." She was thankful she'd managed to sound so strong, because in reality the thought of crawling through that opening gave her the creeps.

"Take it slow," Nicholas encouraged. "Feel first, then inch your way inside."

"Sterling," Grant protested, "I don't like this."

Camille ignored the exchange between the men and did exactly as Nicholas told her. She looked, touched and then inched forward.

It was a tight squeeze for her shoulders but once her upper chest was beyond the opening, the rest of her body slid right through.

Camille settled on her knees and looked around with the aid of the flashlight. No wonder Nicholas remembered this place.

He'd painted scenes all around the walls. Childlike drawings of stick figures and what were obviously the sun and the moon. The cliffs and the ocean.

"What do you see?" Nicholas called out.

Camille sat back on her haunches and stared at the wall. What looked like stories had been etched into the stone. The painted scenes were faded and harder to interpret.

"Camille, tell me what you see," Nicholas repeated.

She chewed her lip while she decided on the best way to sum up the artwork. "There are drawings." She twisted at the waist and slowly roamed the flashlight's beam over the remaining walls. "They're everywhere," she said more to herself than to Nicholas.

"I need to wedge myself through that opening."

She rotated in that direction. She wasn't sure Nicholas had been speaking to her but she felt reasonably sure he wouldn't be able to manage the feat.

"I don't think—"

Before she could finish her argument Nicholas had wriggled his head and shoulders into the opening, but he wasn't getting those broad shoulders through.

After some major grunting and prodding he admitted defeat. "Find a starting point," he instructed, "and tell me what you see."

Easy enough. Camille settled back on her heels and picked a spot. Most of the lower drawings were painted and seriously faded; they didn't appear to have any relevance to anything but a child's imagination.

She got the distinct impression that the drawings nearer to the floor were done by someone very young. The artwork was rudimentary at best.

"Wait." She frowned as she considered one of the final drawings near the floor. "There's one where two stick figures appear to be in water." Was that the ocean or one of the lakes surrounding Raven's Cliff? She couldn't be sure. But it was obvious that one figure was attempting to hold the other under the water. When she told Nicholas as much he didn't respond.

Then she knew the reason why. The next drawing was of the stick figures once more, and one was smeared with paint as if the artist had attempted to obliterate the second figure. Did this have something to do with his murderous twin brother? Maybe she would ask him later, when her baby was safe in her arms.

"Is there more?"

Nicholas's voice was gruff. She doubted he could be comfortable in that position.

"Yes." She moved the light higher on the wall. "The others are etched into the stone as if the artist used a chisel." No more paintings. She scanned the entire niche again. Yep. Just the etchings.

"Study them carefully. Tell me everything you see."

Taking her time, Camille described the chiseled drawings. The effort was tedious and time consuming. She wasn't sure what he thought she would find, but she hoped it was worth the effort.

The hours were ticking down.

"Wait, there's a rhyme or riddle written here." The words, too, were etched into the stone.

"Read them to me," Nicholas urged.

Camille studied the words; some were misspelled or the letters were crooked. Again, this had to be the work of a small child. Probably Nicholas. "Now I lay me down to sleep." She read the words aloud, the resonance of her voice startling her when her brain digested the phrase she'd just spoken. Nicholas had mentioned this bedtime prayer. His grandfather had made up his own version and repeated it to Nicholas every night.

"Keep going," he urged.

She moistened her lips and forged on. "I pray the hollows my soul to keep." Her heart started to pound. Definitely the one his grandfather had inspired. "If I should die before I wake…" Her jaw fell slack when her mind assimilated the rest.

"Camille," he demanded, "what does it say?"

"I pray the hollows my secret will keep safe." She swallowed the emotion clogging her throat and continued, "When life's light fades, I promise to find new life deep in the caves."

Nicholas had been right. *Deep in the caves.* The second lens was here somewhere. That had to be what the words meant.

"You were right," she cried, breathless. "It is here."

"Make sure you haven't missed anything," Nicholas prompted.

Camille stood as best she could. She couldn't straighten completely. Slowly, carefully, she scanned the walls. Drawings and more drawings. She wondered if her son would inherit his father's childhood penchant for art. Or would he inherit his uncle's mental illness. She shuddered at the possibility.

The beam highlighted a row of letters in broad strokes. "Yes." Her heart thumped. "There's more." She sidestepped to get closer to where the new rhyme was written. "Okay. Here we go." Hope swelled in her chest. "Deep, deep in the hole is the key, the key that will set all of Raven's Cliff free."

That had to mean something important. The *key*.

"Camille, don't move."

"What?" She turned toward the opening where Nicholas waited. From where she stood she could no longer see the top of his dark head. "Does that mean something to you?" It had to. Dammit. It had to.

"Don't move."

She shrugged. He'd practically growled

the words. "Okay." The idea that he could have seen something slither across the rocks sent a shudder through her. Did snakes venture this deep into the caves?

Fear trickled into her veins. "If that means what I think it means, you—"

A drop of water plopped against her forehead. She jumped in spite of knowing exactly what it was. "Damn." She swiped her forehead, bumped her elbow against the rock wall and staggered back a step. Her foot slipped off the edge of a rock and before she could regain her balance she went down.

Where was the floor?

Her shoulder bumped a ledge. Down. Way down. She clutched at the wall. A shrill sound bounced off the walls. Her scream.

She hit the ground on her feet. The impact forced her onto her knees.

She shook her head to clear it. Forced her breathing to slow. When she'd gathered her wits and determined that she wasn't dead or seriously injured, she stood, her legs shaky. Her right ankle burned a bit and her shoulder hurt like hell but otherwise she was okay.

"Damn, that was…weird."

She looked up. Nothing but darkness.

That's when she realized that Nicholas and Grant were shouting her name.

"I'm okay," she yelled back. Then she shivered. Snakes. Spiders. There could be lizards. "What the hell am I doing down here?"

She couldn't see a damned thing. Why was there a hole? Okay, dumb question. Caves were full of unexpected holes and detours.

Where had she dropped her flashlight? She crouched down and felt around the floor. Another shudder quaked through her at the idea of what she might find. When her fingers encountered the cool metal of the flashlight she breathed a sigh of relief. The light didn't come on when she pressed the switch. She shook the flashlight, banged it against her palm and the light flickered on.

"That was close." She pushed to her feet, surveyed the area above her. The men were still shouting and maybe arguing among themselves.

"Did you fall into the hole?"

Now he tells her about the hole. "Yes, Nicholas, I fell into the hole."

"Are you sure you're all right?" Grant shouted.

"I'm okay. A little shaken, but okay."

"There are small ledges and niches in the wall. You can climb out using those," Nicholas assured her.

She searched the wall with the light until she found a handhold. "I see what you mean." Great, now she could climb out of here. Considering how out of shape she was, it wouldn't exactly be easy.

"Before you climb up, you need to look for the key."

What? "What key?"

"The key that will set all of Raven's Cliff free."

The rhyme on the wall. A new surge of anticipation charged along her nerve endings. Camille turned around in the hole, scanned the light over the floor. "I…I don't see anything."

"Keep looking, it has to be there."

Okay, she told herself. *Pay attention.*

An inch at a time, she examined the floor, then the walls all the way up to eye level.

Nothing.

"There's no key," she shouted.

"You're sure?"

"I'm…sure." The key must be important. The disappointment was keen in his voice.

A moment passed then he said, "Take your time climbing back up."

Disgusted, Camille dropped her head back and blew out a lungful of air. How was this going to help them find her son? If they couldn't give the kidnapper what he wanted…

"Camille."

She opened her eyes. "Yes."

"One step at a time," Nicholas implored. "Slowly. Okay?"

"Okay."

She tucked the flashlight into her waistband and reached for the first handhold. One toe niche, one handhold at a time, she moved upward. By the time she'd reached the halfway point, her legs and arms were shaking violently.

It wasn't that far, but she'd lain in that hospital bed for so long her muscles weren't up to this kind of challenge.

She reached for the next handhold and her fingers landed on something not a part of the rock.

Her fingers instinctively curled around the object before she could jerk her hand back. Not a creepy crawly. She relaxed and attempted to identify the object.

Metal.

A key.

Adrenaline roared through her.

She rubbed her thumb and forefinger over it again. Definitely a key.

"I found it!"

She'd found the key that would set Raven's Cliff free.

But would it help free her baby?

Chapter Eight

Nicholas held the key in his hand. It could go to anything. There were dozens of possibilities in the house alone. More time.

"You're certain you're all right?" Bridges asked Camille. He'd asked that same question over and over for the past hour.

"I'm fine, really."

Camille had emerged from the cave with a number of scrapes and bruises. She would be sore as hell tomorrow but otherwise she was unharmed.

They had made their way back to the house and rehydrated with bottled water. Nicholas was ready to get started attempting to determine what the key unlocked, but he didn't particularly want Bridges along for this part. As helpful as the man had been thus far, even going so far as to defend Nicholas in town, he couldn't give his trust so easily.

As Nicholas had roamed deeper into the cave, memories had bobbed to the surface. Playing in the passageways. Drawing on the walls of the cave. He and Alex, before his twin had been sent away. Before he'd tried to drown Nicholas. Nicholas had drawn the images he'd foreseen of his brother attempting to hold him under the water. Even as a child he'd sensed his brother's jealousy. Some part of his brother had loved him, Nicholas remembered that as well. Now he would never know the reason Alex had turned evil.

Nicholas pushed the thoughts of his brother aside. Right now he had to find that lens. For Camille and her baby. For his quest. The irony wasn't lost on him that his quest and the search for the child had intertwined.

Fate. Destiny.

The curse.

"We have company," Bridges announced.

Nicholas glanced in the direction Bridges was looking. He was ready to begin his search. He didn't need any distractions. In fact, he would much prefer that Bridges went on his way. Camille could stay…but it would be best if she didn't.

"It's my father," Camille said as she stood beside Bridges and peered out the front window. "This won't be pleasant."

Bridges looked from her to Nicholas. "Why don't Camille and I take this situation back to her house and let you get on with what you need to do." He glanced at his watch. "We'll rendezvous at dark."

Nicholas nodded. "That works for me."

Camille reached into her purse and withdrew her cell phone. "Keep this in case you need to call." She approached Nicholas, the phone in her outstretched palm. "Or, in case *he* calls again."

Nicholas accepted the phone. Since there was no phone in the house and he'd never bothered with a cell, hers would prove useful. "I'll let you know if I find anything." He stared at the innocuous phone. "Or if he calls."

Grant ushered her toward the door. "We should get out there before your father gets out of the car."

Camille nodded. She looked back at

Nicholas once more before Bridges guided her out the front door.

She was counting on Nicholas to find the lens and save her child.

He hoped like hell he was up to the challenge.

Nicholas walked to the window and watched as Perry Wells ranted to Bridges about his daughter's presence at Beacon Manor. Nicholas didn't have to hear the words; he understood how Perry Wells, as well as the rest of Raven's Cliff, felt about him. Bridges could handle Wells. It was Camille who would suffer. She looked ready to drop. She had to be exhausted. All those weeks in the hospital had left her fragile. Today's physical exertion had taken a toll. Nicholas ached to hold her, to comfort her. But that would be selfish of him. She needed a better man than him. As if his thought had somehow telegraphed itself, Grant pulled her to him and kissed her on the forehead. Fury whipped through Nicholas. He battled it back. He had no right.

When both vehicles had driven away, Nicholas began his search. He went through each room of the manor house, tried the key in every lock. The doors, any locking cabinets and pieces of furniture.

Voices from the past whispered in his ears. His mother's soft voice and rare smile. His father's brooding monotone when he was present. He'd spent most of his time traveling on business. Nicholas wondered if his absence was more a statement of how much he'd hated Beacon Manor. The highlights of Nicholas's childhood had been his grandfather's bold laughter and consistent presence.

Nicholas recalled now that after Alex had been taken away he had been lonely. His grandfather had done all he could to keep him happy and occupied. Eventually Nicholas had started school and made friends, and his identical twin had been forgotten. Except for those strange dreams that had plagued Nicholas on and off his whole life.

Nicholas banished the memories. He needed to focus.

There had to be something he was missing.

Room by room, square foot by square foot, he started over. If it took him all night, he would find the lock this key opened.

CAMILLE SAT AS STILL as possible on the sofa. Her parents had assumed their respective chairs. Grant had been encouraged to go home. Only, of course, after her mother had repeatedly told him how he was Camille's saving grace.

"Young lady," Perry Wells began, never a good sign, "we've decided that drastic measures are in order."

Camille stiffened. "What do you mean?"

"Clearly," her mother picked up where her father had left off, "you're not yourself."

Fury rocked through Camille. "And you find that odd? Mother—" Camille leaned forward "—someone held me against my will for months. He drugged me, leaving me no memory of the time. And he waited." She swallowed, but the emotion jammed in her throat would not be dismissed so easily. "Waited until my baby was born and he took him. Then he left me for dead on the street." She blinked at the tears brimming. Damn it. She did not want to cry. "In the rain. Had Detective Lagios not found me when he did, we likely would not be having this conversation."

Her parents exchanged a look Camille

knew all too well. They were convinced she was wrong about all or part of her story.

"I know you don't believe me," she hazarded to add. "But it's the truth. If—" Camille stopped herself. She could not divulge the ransom call. Not yet. Not until Nicholas had done all within his power to meet the man's demands. She wasn't sure how the kidnapper could know if they contacted the police but she wasn't willing to take the risk. Not yet.

"Camille, sweetheart," Beatrice Wells patronized, "we're worried about your mental health. There's no way to know the long-term effects of the drugs you were given. At the very least you should be in counseling."

Oh, God. She got it now. They wanted to label her behavior, along with her, as mentally unstable. "I'm not crazy," she snapped.

What were they thinking? She couldn't sit here and allow them to treat her like a child. The next thing she knew they would have her locked away in some ritzy resort-type mental institution. She knew her parents too well. They would do anything to save face.

"No one is saying you're crazy, honey,"

her father insisted. "Like your mother said, we're worried about you. Look at you." He gestured vaguely at her. "Your cheek is bruised. Your hands are scratched. Your clothes are filthy. What on earth have you been doing?"

"I've been searching for my baby," she said, her body beginning to quake visibly.

Another of those knowing looks passed between her parents.

"Do you expect me to sit here and do nothing?" She launched to her feet. "Good grief, Mother, how would you have felt if I or Corrine had gone missing as an infant? Would you have lounged around the house waiting for someone else to bring me to you?"

Her father patted the air with both hands, signaling for her to retake her seat. "We have people working on finding your baby. You know that. I've offered a large reward. The child will be found. Soon."

He just didn't know.

Camille looked from her father to her mother and then shook her head. "It's not going to be that simple."

Her mother heaved a beleaguered breath.

"How do you know? You don't even know who held you or where. That's why it's so important to let the professionals handle this. We simply don't know how to go about this sort of thing."

"I'm going to take a shower." Camille turned to go, but her father stood, making her pause.

"That's a good idea, honey." He flared his hands as if he knew in advance that what he was about to say wouldn't sit well with her. "But be aware, we've asked Dr. Kline to stop by and have an informal session with you."

"Who is Dr. Kline?" She wasn't the one who was crazy. Her parents were! Camille was a grown woman. She didn't have to put up with this.

Her mother pushed to her feet. "Dr. Kline is driving all the way from Portland. He's the best psychiatrist in New England. He's only going to talk to you, Camille. What harm could come of that?"

"Is he bringing a straitjacket with him?" This was nuts. "Men in white suits?" She backed away from the people she had trusted her entire life. "I am appalled that you would treat me like a child. Or worse, like a mental case. I am not crazy. I'm desperate to find my child." She bumped into the door frame leading to the hall. "If you continue treating me this way I'll have no choice but to leave."

With that she turned her back and headed to her room. It didn't matter whether they continued along this path or not. Camille was leaving. She couldn't trust her parents not to take even more ludicrous steps. She could wake up in an institution. Her father had been a very powerful man for a very long time. He knew people in high places. And, obviously, in low places.

Her best bet would be to stay away from her parents until this was done.

Until she had her baby back.

BY THE TIME CAMILLE had showered and packed her bag, her parents' company had arrived. Her room was at the back of the house, so she couldn't see if a vehicle had arrived. But she could hear the lowered voices.

This could get ugly.

Camille wished that Grant were still here. He would defend her.

Nicholas would defend her, too.

But once the lens was found and she had her baby back, depending upon Nicholas for anything would be a mistake. She'd been down that path before. He'd abandoned her. He'd bent to the will of his father and forsaken her and what they had shared.

Camille picked up her overnight bag and purse, braced herself and emerged from her room. As she walked along the hall toward the living room, the voices grew more distinct. Her mother, her father and another male.

The infamous Dr. Kline.

Her father had surely pulled some major strings to have such a prestigious doctor pay a house call all the way from Portland.

For the first time she seriously wished her parents' home had an entry hall. But it didn't, so she had no choice but to exit through the living room. If she used the back door they would surely use the front, reaching her car first. She hoped it wouldn't come to that, but she wasn't taking the chance.

The conversation hushed when she entered the room. Her mother took one look at the bag in her hand and gasped. The color drained from her father's face. The visitor—Dr. Kline, she presumed—merely smiled.

"Hello, Camille." He stood. "I'm Dr. Kline."

"I'm sorry you've driven all this way for nothing, Doctor." Camille looked to Beatrice. "Mother." Then to Perry. "Father, I need a few days to myself. You can call my cell if you need to reach me."

"Camille."

She shouldn't have stopped when the doctor called her name.

"Perry, do something," her mother groused.

Camille shouldn't have turned around at her mother's comment. But she did.

"Mother, there is nothing you or Father can do. I'm leaving. I'll be fine. I don't need your kind of help."

"I'm certain you're distraught," Kline persisted.

Distraught? Camille glared at the man. "I'm not distraught, Dr. Kline, I'm devastated. But I'm not going to let that stop me from finding my baby."

"This is likely the most difficult challenge you'll face in your life, Camille."

At least he'd gotten that part right.

"As hard as it is to consider all the avenues, there are many that need to be explored."

What the hell was he talking about?

"It's not unusual for a young, first-time mother to change her mind. To feel the child will be a burden or will somehow change her life in a way that would lead to unhappiness. We can explore your feelings and determine what really happened."

Camille couldn't respond to that. She walked out the door and straight to her car. She wouldn't be back. Not until her parents realized that she had not harmed her child. Or given him away.

First she drove to her house. Her parents had had the power and water turned off while she was gone. The house was dark and closed up like a mausoleum. Camille couldn't stay there.

She couldn't go to Grant. He had given up his apartment right before their wedding day and was still living at Cliffside Inn. She prayed he wasn't hoping their relationship would resume. When this was over and she had her baby back, they had to have a serious talk.

That left Beacon Manor.

Though spending time alone with Nicholas

was not smart, she needed to be with him right now to get through the next thirty-six hours. To ensure all that could be was being done.

Camille turned her car around and headed toward the lighthouse. Whether he liked it or not, he was going to have a houseguest his first night back at Beacon Manor.

They would spend the night looking for the necessary clues to find the lens. There would be no time for trouble.

She should have thought of this plan earlier.

They'd planned to rendezvous at dark anyway.

Beacon Manor seemed the perfect place.

NICHOLAS STOOD OUTSIDE in the cold night. Fall was heavy in the air but he didn't care about the chill. He'd found nothing the key opened.

He stared at the watch room that lay in absolute darkness. Where had those rare stones come from? How had Captain Raven, the founder of Raven's Cliff, discovered such stones? Could a mere stone possibly possess mystical powers? For that matter, was the curse simply a state of mind?

On some level Nicholas wanted to forget the whole matter. To pretend his quest wouldn't make any difference in the fate of the village or any one person's life. That the curse indeed only existed in the minds of those who wanted to believe.

But Camille's missing child would not allow him to be so cavalier. There was something dark and evil going on here. That a man had made the ransom call changed nothing. Evil worked through humans.

Nicholas could feel the evil at work here. Despite the downfall of the terrorists and the Seaside Strangler and the fool who had killed so many with his poison fish, the heaviness of pure malevolence lingered like a killing stench in the very air he breathed.

A jolt of adrenaline soared through Nicholas's veins. He jerked with the force of it. Brilliant pinpoints of light burned his eyes. The pain sliced through his brain, forced him to his knees.

When his vision returned it was blurry. He tried to lift his hands to swipe his eyes but couldn't move. He opened his mouth to cry out but couldn't speak. His heart thundered, threatening its confines.

An obscured image filtered onto the screen that was his retinas.

A man…his back was turned so that Nicholas could not see his face at all, not even his profile. The man was bent over something…a bed…no, a…cradle.

Nicholas's heart rammed against his sternum. A baby lay in the cradle. Eyes closed in sleep. A shock of dark hair against the white linens taunted Nicholas, stole his breath.

His child.

Nicholas knew with complete certainty that the infant in the cradle was his child.

Camille's child.

The man moved away from the cradle. He passed through a doorway, then walked slowly down a long, dimly lit corridor.

White walls.

High ceilings.

The image blurred. Nicholas closed his eyes. Tried to see more.

But it was gone.

Air burst into his lungs.

Nicholas coughed, then wheezed.

When his legs felt steady enough he stood. Rubbed the back of his hand over his eyes. He blinked once, twice.

He'd seen Camille's baby.

And the man.

But the image had been indistinct and grainy, like watching an old black-and-white movie.

But the infant lived.

Somewhere close.

Nicholas could still feel his presence. He could smell the soft baby skin. He inhaled deeply, the sweet scent playing havoc with his heart.

Lights flickered in the distance. Nicholas dragged his thoughts from the vision and squinted to make out the vehicle approaching.

A car. Blue in color.

Camille's car.

The car stopped and she climbed from behind the wheel. He remembered then that he was going to try to call her.

The memory of the vision he'd experienced, the baby sleeping in the cradle, knotted his gut.

Camille had been right. Her baby was alive. And it was a boy.

His son.

Nicholas shook with the weight of it.

Camille reached into the backseat and then closed the door. As she approached him Nicholas realized she carried a bag. An overnight bag.

She'd come to stay.

With him.

At Beacon Manor.

Chapter Nine

"You can't have checked every lock," Camille argued, her desperation hitting a new high.

"Every single one." Nicholas turned his back to her and stared into the flickering flames of the fire. With no electricity he'd had to gather wood and start a fire in the parlor's massive fireplace to chase away the autumn chill. He'd lit a couple of kerosene lanterns and several candles to keep the darkness at bay.

He exhaled a heavy sigh. "The key doesn't fit any of the locks in the house."

Camille hugged her arms around her waist and fought the urge to cry. They were running out of time. If they didn't find the lens soon…

She shuddered, couldn't allow herself to think the worst. They had to find the lens. There was no other choice.

The distinct chirp of her cell phone jerked her from the terrifying thought. "That's my phone," she said, moving across the room, toward where Nicholas lingered by the fireplace.

He reached into the pocket of his jeans and withdrew the phone. She took it from his hand before he could open it. The display read, *1 new message.*

A text.

Her fingers trembled when she opened the phone to read the text message.

You are running out of time.

The bastard had read her mind. Her entire body started to shake, only this time with anger. "We have to find that lens." She shoved the phone at Nicholas and stormed to the window that looked out to the ocean.

She didn't have to see the shore to know that the frothy water would be bashing against the rocks the same way her anger was blasting her senses. There was no news from the police. Nothing from the FBI or the private investigator her father had hired.

No one knew anything except the man who had her son.

And he wanted just one thing.

The lens.

What kind of person used an innocent baby as leverage? Who was this man?

Nicholas moved up beside her. Camille couldn't look at him. If she did, she would never be able to hold back the tears already burning her eyes. That he remained silent told her he didn't know what to say. Her chest seized. What could he say? Nothing. There was nothing to say. Time was running out and they had no idea where to look for the next clue. They had nothing.

Stop. She had to think. If she gave up now…what kind of mother gave up at all? Renewed determination fired through her veins. She would not give up.

Lifting her chin in defiance of the emotions waging a war inside her, she turned to him. "If this key is the one that will set Raven's Cliff free—" she cleared her throat in an attempt to steady her voice "—why doesn't it fit one of the locks?"

"I tried every piece of furniture, every

door…" He sighed. "I don't know the answer."

Camille reached for patience, kept the initial response to herself. This wasn't Nicholas's fault. He was a victim in this the same as she was. She wondered vaguely where Grant was. Waiting for her to call, she supposed. Maybe he was too tired to continue helping in the search. Or maybe he'd realized that he owed her nothing and that he should just cut his losses.

Camille covered her face with her hands and pressed against her eyes with her fingertips to ward off the fresh wave of tears. Damn it. She did not want to cry. She wanted to be strong.

"There must be something we're missing," Nicholas suggested as if he understood she was falling into deep despair once more. He touched her arm. A whisper of heat warmed her.

She dropped her hands to her sides and pushed away the overwhelming emotions, including the need his nearness generated. He was right. They had to be missing something. Now was not the time to fall apart.

"We won't give up until we find it."

Nicholas squeezed her arm before stepping away. He started to pace the large room, the steady fall of his soles on the wood floor amping up the tension already thick in the air.

She didn't want to, but she desperately needed him now. All she had to do was hold it together. And to think. Think! They needed to be doing something!

She closed her eyes and softly recited the words she'd read in the cave room. *"I pray the hollows my secret will keep safe. When life's light fades, I promise to find new life deep in the caves. Deep, deep in the hole is the key, the key that will set all of Raven's Cliff free."*

"We have the key," Nicholas said just as softly. "There has to be more to the riddle."

Maybe they already had the answer and just didn't know it. Camille opened her eyes. "Recite that prayer or whatever your grandfather told you every night."

Nicholas stopped pacing, that fierce blue gaze settled on hers. *"Now I lay me down to sleep. I pray the hollows my soul to keep. If I should die before I wake, I pray the hollows my secret will keep safe."*

It was Camille's turn to pace now. "We figured out that the hollows were the caves." She shoved a handful of curly hair behind her ear. "We found the hole and the key. What's next?" She stopped and looked at Nicholas. "If the key doesn't fit any of the locks in the house, where else can we try?" The property had a couple of other buildings, including a barn. "There have to be other locks on the estate."

He considered her suggestion for what felt like forever before shaking his head. "There are no locks that require a key like this in the old carriage house or the barn."

Adrenaline singed her skin as she had an epiphany. "What about the lighthouse?"

He moved his head side to side again. "Nothing—" He hesitated, then said, "Well, maybe…"

"Nicholas?" Her heart started to beat faster.

"There's one possibility…" A distant look claimed his eyes as if he were remembering something from deep in his past. "Yes. There is one possibility."

"What?" He was killing her!

"The lantern." He scrubbed his hand over the damaged side of his face. *"Maybe."*

The lantern. Of course. "What're we waiting for?" She turned to head for the door.

"Wait."

At the door Camille paused long enough to turn back to him. "Hurry, Nicholas."

"The fire did a lot of damage to the upper portion of the staircase and the watch room. It isn't safe."

"I don't care." Camille gave him her back and kept walking. "I'm going up there." Urgency propelled her. No way was she letting anything stop her. Any possibility was better than none at all...no matter the danger involved.

She didn't slow down until she was out the front door and headed down the steps. She wouldn't have slowed even then if Nicholas hadn't caught her by the arm.

"Camille, listen to me."

His grip was like a vise; there was no escaping, but she tried anyway. "Let me go, Nicholas. We don't have time to argue about this."

"Listen, please." He manacled her other arm and gave her a gentle shake. "The fire did structural damage. The flooring up there could give way under our weight. This lighthouse is old. The entire structure is wood. No metal supports were added in the last century or so as has been the case with so many other lighthouses."

She glared into his stern gaze. Even with nothing more than the moonlight it was impossible to miss the intensity there. "If there's any chance the answer to this puzzle is up there, I'm going. Don't try to stop me."

"Both of us don't need to go," he countered. He released her left arm and fished the cell phone out of his pocket. "Keep the phone to call for help if…something happens."

He was going up there. No matter that it was dangerous. Would the old Nicholas have done something so selfless? She shook her head. The past had no place in this. He was going, but he wasn't going alone. "I'm going with you."

For one long moment their gazes remained locked in battle. She expected him to argue.

"All right," he relented, to her surprise. "But you stay five steps behind me. If I tell you to go back, you do it. No questions."

She nodded. "Whatever you say."

Nicholas looked up at the lighthouse. "We'll need the lanterns."

"I'll get them." Camille tugged her arm free of his hold and rushed back into the house. She grabbed both the battery-operated lantern and one of the kerosene ones Nicholas had found in the house.

When she got outside once more he was already striding toward the looming structure that had towered over all of Raven's Cliff since its establishment more than two centuries ago.

At the entry on the ground level Nicholas took the kerosene lantern. "Remember—" he held her gaze with his, allowed her to see the determination there "—stay at least five steps behind me as we go up. At the first sign of trouble, turn back. No arguments."

Her fingers tightened around the handle of the lantern she held. "No arguments."

Stepping inside that soaring structure had the effect of an ever-tightening band around her chest. If legend were to be believed, this lighthouse was the key to Raven's Cliff's prosperity as well as its despair. For as long as she could remember, Beacon Manor and its lighthouse had been a major part of her life. The idea that the clue they needed might be found here somehow made a strange kind of sense.

Despite the passage of five years the interior of the lighthouse still smelled of smoke and charred wood. The recent rains had dampened the decaying interior, ripening the smell. Camille's heart pounded harder as she climbed the first step, taking care to stay well behind Nicholas as ordered.

He'd climbed scarcely a dozen steps when the ancient wood began to creak forebodingly beneath his weight. He paused, glanced back at her a lingering moment before continuing upward. Camille prayed with all her might as they continued upward. They had to reach that lantern. If there was any chance a clue to the location of the lens was hidden there, they had to take this risk.

She kept the fingers of one hand firmly wrapped around the narrow safety rail. It was a little shaky but she held on to her courage. She had to be strong.

Higher and higher they climbed. Nicholas hesitated on each step, testing his weight there before continuing upward. Her breath grew ragged from the exertion or perhaps from the anticipation or a combination of the two. More than twelve hours had passed, which meant less than thirty-six remained.

Her arms ached to hold her baby close.

Finally the last five steps lay before her. Nicholas paused on the landing of the watch room to wait for her. Her mouth went abruptly dry. She'd gotten used to the odor of devastation, but it was what her eyes saw that ripped at her already-ravaged emotions. Jagged shards were all that remained of the wall of glass that had encircled the watch room. The roar of the ocean ramming the rocks below somehow sounded louder here. The blackened wood floor and disabled lantern that waited helplessly in the dark represented death as surely as any corpse she'd ever seen.

The sadness was overwhelming. Dense in the air.

"I want you to wait right here."

Nicholas's voice jerked her from the troubling thoughts. She blinked, assimilated what he meant. "Okay." He wanted her to wait near the winding staircase in case she needed to go for help. Considering the condition of the floor, she had no problem with that.

The old-fashioned lantern sat next to what had been the lens. It wasn't as large as most she'd seen. Some of the more up-to-date lighthouses were equipped with a lens that weighed thousands of pounds and sent light more than twenty miles out to sea. What was left of this lens frame was far, far smaller. A person could easily pick it up and carry it. How could something so small have been responsible for the piercing beam of light she recalled seeing as a child?

Perhaps the lens had been something mystical or magical.

Focus, Camille. Stay out of the past. "Do you see a lock?"

"I don't know yet." After studying the lantern a moment more, he paused on the far side, making it difficult for her to see what he had found. That he reached into his pocket for the key sent hope exploding in her veins.

"Did you find something?"

"I think so."

He worked for long minutes on one section of the lantern. Eventually the screech of metal on metal told her he had discovered an opening. Her pulse reacted.

"The key unlocks a small access panel beneath the maintenance door." He shook his head. "I never noticed that before."

She moved a step in his direction. "Maybe you weren't supposed to." The thought came out of nowhere, but somehow it felt right. "What do you see?" She couldn't bear the tension a second longer.

He glanced over at her. "Don't come any closer."

"Okay, okay." She crossed her arms over her chest. "Just tell me what you see."

He turned his attention back to the lantern. "There's an inscription on the back of the panel." He held up his lantern to get a better look.

The pounding behind Camille's sternum had blood roaring so loudly that she could scarcely hear, much less breathe.

Please, please let the answer be there.

"Salvation lies inside you." Nicholas heaved a frustrated breath. "What the hell does that mean?"

"Is that all it says?" She was rushing

toward the lantern before the action registered in her brain.

"I told you to stay at the landing," he barked.

"I can't." She didn't stop until she was next to him. "I have to see."

The scrolled letters spelled out exactly what he'd said and nothing more. The hope drained out of her, leaving her weak and more terrified than she could ever recall being. How were they going to find that damned lens if they couldn't figure out this stupid riddle?

No giving up. She studied the tarnished brass of the massive lantern. There had to be more.

"We shouldn't stay up here too long," Nicholas urged. "It isn't safe."

The wind howled hauntingly and the fog was rolling in, but Camille didn't care. She needed to find something, anything that would give them some sort of direction on where to go from here.

"Camille." He reached for her hand, clasped it firmly. "Let's go."

When she would have argued, something snagged her attention. She leaned closer, noticed what looked like more engraved words. Pulling the sleeve of her shirt over the heel of her hand she rubbed and rubbed until the soot cleared.

"There's more." Her pulse jumped. "Deep in the hollows of the heart so proud…you will find the treasure you seek."

More words and yet they told them nothing. This was impossible. Camille scrubbed the back of her hand over her face and tried to make sense of the words. "Does that mean anything to you?"

When Nicholas didn't immediately respond, she snapped, "It's nothing but the same message as before, isn't it? *Salvation lies inside you.* Great!" She turned her back and headed to the staircase. They weren't going to get any answers here. She should just call the FBI and let them try to find this bastard.

She and Nicholas were getting nowhere fast.

"Watch your step, Camille," he warned.

She just wanted out of here. This whole exercise had been one of futility. She was no closer to finding her baby now than she had been twelve hours ago. Nicholas's grandfather had obviously harbored a sick sense of humor. There wasn't a damned thing funny about his ridiculous riddles. She was sick. Sick of the curse. Sick of not knowing where her baby was and if he was okay.

As soon as Camille was back on solid ground she was calling Chief Swanson. No more playing this crazy game. She couldn't keep pretending they had a chance.

Clearly they didn't.

Time was running out.

"Camille, slow down!"

Until he said the words, she hadn't been aware of her hasty movements. Her right foot hit the next step at that same instant…only it didn't stop. The wood gave way and she lunged forward.

Time moved in slow motion as she somehow watched the lantern she'd been holding tumble end over end, down, down, down until it crashed onto the floor far below. Strangely, she was following its path.

Her momentum abruptly halted. Pain seared through her shoulder.

"Camille! Look at me!"

Several more seconds were required before she understood that Nicholas wanted her to look up at him. He held on to the railing with one hand, the other was wrapped around one of her wrists. She studied his tightly clenched fingers where they bit into her skin, then followed the length of her arm where it connected with her body. Something wasn't right.

"Look at me, Camille!"

Her gaze latched back on to his. What was happening?

"I need you to reach up and grab hold of my arm with your other hand."

Her other hand? She looked down her other arm, considered the hand hanging limply at her side. Then she saw her legs…her feet.

They dangled in the air. Not on the steps! *In the air*…with nothing but more air…all the way to the floor where the lantern had shattered.

Fear throttled through her.

She was going to fall.

Her baby was lost to her.

And she was going to die.

Now.

Who would take care of her baby boy if she died?

Her eyes sought and found Nicholas's. Would he take care of their son?

The skin where he clutched her arm burned while the muscle beneath felt like ice...numb.

"You have to listen to me, Camille," he commanded. "Reach up and grab my arm. Now!"

Yes, she needed to do as he said. Her body remained paralyzed. Move! She ordered her arm to move. It refused. Sweat broke out across her forehead. "Oh, God." She swallowed at the fear clogging her throat.

She was going to die.

"Hurry, Camille," Nicholas urged. "Reach up."

"Promise me, Nicholas," she cried. "Promise me you'll find our baby and take care of him." Her shoulder stung, burned.

"Camille—"

"Promise!"

Fear, stark and vivid, lit in his eyes. "I promise. Now, reach up and take my hand."

Somehow her hand moved upward. Camille watched in morbid fascination as if she had no control over the limb reaching up or the fingers taking hold of his arm.

Then her body was moving upward, as well. Nicholas grunted with the effort of hauling her up. Her chest hit the edge of a wooden step.

She let loose of Nicholas and grabbed at the step. He roared, the sound raw, as he dragged her back onto the steps next to him.

Her body shook so hard she was certain she would fall again, but he pulled her into his arms and held her so tight that there was no way she would fall. She couldn't say how long he held her that way—hours…maybe only minutes.

The one thing she knew for certain was that she had not felt this safe in so very long. Only Nicholas had ever made her feel complete and protected. And he had promised to take care of their baby. He had promised.

"Can you walk?"

She nodded, brushed the hair from her face. Her cheeks were damp. She was crying. How could she be crying and not know it? "I…" She cleared her throat. "I can walk."

"Let's take it slow."

One creaking step at a time they completed the journey downward. Nicholas held on tight, never allowing her to be more than a few inches from him.

When they were outside again, she collapsed onto the ground, her legs no longer able to hold her weight.

"You're okay now," he murmured as he knelt beside her. He cradled her in his strong arms and assured her over and over again that she was safe.

The sobs came then. She tried to stop them but there was no way her emotions would be contained a moment longer. Months of her life were missing. Her baby was missing. And she was helpless. She had failed to keep her child safe, failed to keep herself safe.

Her whole life was one huge failure.

The landscape was moving. It took a moment for her to realize that Nicholas had lifted her into his arms and was carrying her toward the mansion. She shivered, only then noticing how cold the wind was. The fog had closed in around them like a suffocating curtain. She squeezed her eyes shut. She didn't want to see. Didn't want to feel. She only wanted to escape. To somehow wake up and find that her life was pieced back together. That her baby was in her arms.

Nicholas kicked the front door closed once they were inside. He carried her to the sofa in the parlor and gently placed her there. "I'm not sure there's anything to drink, but I'll see what I can find."

Her eyes closed once more and she ordered her head to stop spinning. She needed to pull herself back together. Falling apart wasn't going to help. Her body ached from her near-death experience. She shuddered then winced at the ferocious pain in her shoulder. This whole business was totally screwed up. Why did this man want the lens? Why kidnap her and take her baby? It didn't make sense. What did she or her child have to do with the lens? Did this bastard somehow know that the child belonged to Nicholas?

That was impossible. No one knew. Only she and Grant. And neither of them had had any idea that a second lens even existed or that it was somehow important or valuable.

"I found some brandy." Nicholas settled on the sofa next to her. "You'll have to drink straight from the bottle. I couldn't find a glass."

Who needed a glass? Camille gladly downed a hefty swig. The burn stole her breath. Good. She chugged another. She wanted this horrible feeling to go away.

"I think that's probably enough." Nicholas tugged the bottle from her hands. "I don't need you to pass out on me."

She stared into his eyes, tried to read what he was thinking. "What difference does it make?" She licked her lips, couldn't help staring at his. He had such beautiful lips. Her gaze roved from his mouth to the damaged side of his face. Even disfigured as he was, he was still...

"What?" She frowned, certain he had said something else to her. His lips had been moving, but she had been caught up in staring at him.

"I said," he repeated, his impatience audible, "I'm going to need your help."

Camille shook her head to clear it. She shouldn't have taken that last slug of brandy. "I don't understand. We're at an impasse. We have nothing." Tears welled inside her once more. She was never going to find her baby. She had failed.

"I think I understand what the message means."

Her gaze locked with his. "What?" Her heart jumped. "What do we do now?" If he had deciphered the message then surely he knew where to start looking next.

"My grandfather always referred to Beacon Manor as his heart. He knew in time that the estate would become mine." Nicholas shrugged. "Then it would be my heart."

Renewed anticipation rushed through Camille. "You're saying the lens is somewhere in this house?"

He nodded. "There's nowhere else it could be."

Camille looked around the enormous room, hope burgeoning. "We'd better get started then."

Beacon Manor was one hell of a big house.

Chapter Ten

"I tried to call Grant," Camille announced as Nicholas entered the kitchen, "but there's no answer."

Nicholas placed the ax and the hammer he'd located on the counter. "Did you leave a message?" It was after midnight. Bridges was likely in bed. Nicholas hated that some part of him relished the idea that Bridges wasn't here when Camille needed him most.

"I did." Camille picked up the hammer. "What're we doing with these?"

"Deep in the hollows of the heart so proud," Nicholas repeated part of the last clue they'd found. He picked up the ax, tested its weight in his hand. "If the heart so proud is this house, then the hollows have to mean either the basement, the attic or the walls."

"So you're going to start busting open walls?" She stared at the hammer in her hand for emphasis.

"If we find nothing in the basement or attic, then we'll do what we have to."

Nicholas had searched the entire house when he'd looked for locks the key might fit. Every box, every cabinet, every piece of furniture had already been explored. If the lens was in the house it had to be inside a wall or hidden cavity. That would be just like his grandfather to have the lens tucked away inside some secret hiding place that only he knew about.

Now that he'd had time to think about it, his grandfather had told him stories about how pirates had hidden treasures inside the walls of houses exactly like this one along the coast of Maine. He'd never mentioned Beacon Manor as being one with secret passages or such hiding places. But the stories themselves may have been a clue he hadn't understood at the time.

Only one way to find out.

In a few hours he and Camille would reach the halfway mark in their specified time limit.

There was no time to waste. If wrecking the plaster in every room of his family home was necessary, then so be it. The plaster would simply join the multitude of other renovations that needed to be accomplished.

"Where do we start?" Camille faced him, hammer in hand, shoulders squared and ready.

"At the top." He grabbed a lantern and gestured for her to grab the other. The fall had damaged the one from the general store, but the kerosene lanterns were good to go for several hours more.

She followed him up the two flights of stairs and then through the door that led to the narrow winding staircase leading to the attic level. On the roof was the widow's walk but there were no hiding places other than the floor of the walk itself. Considering that storms had ripped the walk apart on more than one occasion, Nicholas doubted that his grandfather would employ the area as a hiding place for something so important.

At the top of the narrow attic stairs Nicholas opened the door that led into the sprawling space. One large room that spanned the length of the entire house. The windows on each end allowed the meager moonlight to filter inside. During the day sunlight would create interesting shadows in the attic. As a kid Nicholas had created many a tall tale related to those shadows.

"You take that side." Nicholas pointed to his left. "I'll take this one."

Since the knee walls had access doors, it wasn't necessary to bust open plaster. He used the lantern to check the wide, low-ceilinged area. Nothing but abandoned pieces of small furniture and a few trunks packed with old clothes and pictures of people he didn't know. A kid-size rocking chair he'd used until he'd been about five sat collecting dust.

Satisfied there was nothing to find, he withdrew from the cramped area and wandered through the attic proper, checking boxes and pieces of furniture again despite the thoroughness of his first search.

"Nothing." Camille dusted her knees with one hand as she pushed into a standing position next to the access door on her side of the attic.

"Okay." Nicholas glanced around one last time. "Down to the second floor."

Room by room, wall by wall, Nicholas and Camille covered the entire second floor. Not a piece of furniture, a closet or box went unchecked. The lack of insulation in the walls made the job easier and reminded Nicholas that his renovations were going to have to include making the house far more energy efficient.

As carefully and extensively as they searched, they still found nothing.

Back on the first floor, Camille collapsed on the parlor sofa. "What if there's nothing down here either?" She looked around, the daunting and fruitless task obviously testing her strength and endurance.

The search and the early hour were taking a terrible toll on her. He reminded himself that she'd given birth only a few weeks ago. Not to mention she'd been seriously ill and bedridden in a hospital for weeks on top of that. She was in no condition to be putting herself through this kind of physical and mental stress.

He should have taken that into account hours ago.

"Why don't you rest here while I keep

looking?" He knew it wouldn't do any good to ask, but he had to try. "If I find anything I'll yell."

She pushed to her feet as he had known she would. "I'm ready."

That he hadn't answered her question didn't seem to matter. She wanted to keep going. It was, unfortunately, their only option at this point.

"We'll take it one room at a time, just like the second floor."

She surveyed the parlor. "I'll start in here."

He nodded, his respect for her growing. He'd always known Camille was kind, compassionate and trustworthy. But in the past few days he'd seen a resilience in her that he hadn't known existed. For a woman who'd been raised with a silver spoon in her mouth she had grit. "I'll begin at the back of the house."

Nicholas checked the mudroom first, then the kitchen. His progress was far faster than Camille's since he had the ax. He could cut through the layer of plaster and then the wooden lathes in half the time her hammer accomplished the job. Again, they went room by room, wall by wall. And found basically nothing but empty, hollow cavities beneath the ancient plaster. Occasionally an old boot or piece of stoneware or page from a newspaper would be discovered. But no lens. And no additional clues.

He didn't have to see the worry in Camille's eyes to know she was losing hope. The slowness of her movements and the sag of her shoulders told him that doubt and fear were creeping back in, overtaking her strength and determination.

Pretty soon even he would have to admit defeat if they didn't find something…anything. They were running out of walls to tear into. The walls in the entry hall were the only ones not sporting gaping holes at this point. When they'd gone over the house from top to bottom there was no place left to look.

"We need coffee." It was four in the morning and he had to admit that he was feeling the burden of weariness as well. He doubted any of the shops in the village would be open at this hour. The one café didn't open for breakfast until closer to six. Since there was no electricity here and his cottage was history, he was relatively sure they were out of luck.

Camille plopped her lantern on the floor and settled onto a step at the bottom of the stairs. "Wishful thinking."

Her voice sounded thin and frail. His chest ached at the sound. He set his lantern next to hers. "Don't give up yet. There's still the basement."

She said nothing to his comment.

The need to reassure her was a palpable force inside him. "My grandfather used to tell me stories about the pirates who took advantage of this coast, the houses as well as the caves, for concealing their pillaged goods." Nicholas wasn't so sure the stories were entirely accurate, or even true for that matter, but he couldn't bear to see her hopes continue to wane. Strange, for most of his life he had worried about no one but himself. Now all he could think about was making things right for her.

Her gaze collided with his; she searched his eyes for so long that he wondered if she had any intention of saying whatever was on her mind. "You mean the stories about the secret passageways and hidden treasures?"

No one grew up on the New England coast

without hearing the pirate stories. Nicholas smiled. "Those are the ones."

She closed her eyes and shook her head, but the corners of her mouth were tilted in the slightest smile. "You didn't really believe all those stories we heard as kids, did you?"

"Some." He smiled then. When her eyes opened once more he couldn't say there was a twinkle in them, but there was definitely a flicker of hope. "We'll find the lens, Camille. And then we'll get your baby back. You have my word. I won't stop until I find him."

For the first time in a very, very long time, Nicholas needed to hold her. Not just wanted to, *needed* to. But he didn't dare. As the moment drew out, tension roared through his body, making him ache to lean closer, making him burn to taste her sweet lips.

"I need you to kiss me, Nicholas."

Her whispered plea was his undoing. He couldn't have said no, couldn't have resisted if his life had depended upon it.

He leaned in, let his lips brush hers. She shivered. Made the sweetest sound. Then he kissed her. Just a soft, chaste meeting of the lips. The sensation sent desire rushing through him. His body tightened in an acutely sexual reaction.

She touched his face. Not the smooth undamaged side, but the ugly, ravaged side. He started to draw away but her other hand curled around his neck and held him still. Gentle fingers traced the hideous scars while her intent gaze followed their path. His heart thumped hard, then harder still. He wanted to bolt. To hide his ugliness from her beauty. Having her look at him when they argued or discussed the plan to find the lens was one thing, but this was different...this was too close...too intimate. His body didn't seem to care that she surely found him repulsive to look at. His muscles hardened. Need heated his blood.

"I don't see this when I look at you," she murmured. Her gaze connected fully with his. "I only see you. The man I loved so much for so long."

"And I let you down," he responded gruffly. "I let everyone down."

She blinked. Her hands fell away. "Yes. You did."

Nicholas rose. Stepped away from her. His traitorous body throbbed with the need she had elicited. Was he out of his mind? Had he not hurt her enough? He had no right to enjoy a tender moment with her...now or ever.

"We should—"

A pounding on the front door cut off his words. He frowned. Who the hell—

"Sterling? Camille?"

Bridges.

"Grant?"

Camille shot to her feet and rushed to the door as if the man on the other side had come to rescue her from the beast and his evil intentions.

Nicholas closed his eyes and cleared his head. He could not allow his foolish emotions to distract him from what he was here to do. Not only did Camille and her child's well-being depend on his finding the lens, Raven's Cliff's future hung in the balance as well.

Whatever had been between him and Camille was long over. She owed him nothing. Clearly she still had feelings for Bridges. As well she should. He was a far better man than Nicholas.

She deserved better.

Her child deserved better.

"Darling, are you all right?" Bridges hugged Camille, but his gaze settled on Nicholas. "Sterling."

"We found what we believe to be another clue," Nicholas said, pushing aside everything but the task at hand. They had no time for anything else.

Camille pulled out of the other man's arms. "We've been looking in the walls and—" she shrugged as she glanced around the massive entry hall "—just about any other possible hiding place. We're down to this room, with nothing but the basement left to search."

Bridges reached for her hammer, then handed her the keys to his car. "I brought a thermos of coffee and some pastries. I had a feeling the two of you had worked through the night. Why don't you get the refreshments and I'll carry on here."

Camille accepted his keys. "God, thank you." She glanced at Nicholas, her cheeks flushed. "We were just saying how coffee would be really good about now."

As she hurried out to Bridges's car, Nicholas wondered if she felt embarrassed that she'd allowed him to kiss her. Asked him to, actually.

Did she regret that impulsive act now that the man she'd intended to marry was here?

Bridges held his arms wide apart and offered a repentant expression. "I'm sorry I wasn't here sooner. I sat down for just a moment and the next thing I knew it was three in the morning." He made a sound that wasn't quite a laugh. "I'm surprised you two haven't collapsed. I don't know how you've kept going."

Nicholas had nothing to say to that. He turned his back to Bridges and picked a spot on the wall, then swung his ax until he'd opened a big enough hole to inspect the cavity beyond the plaster and lathes.

One by one he inspected the cavities between the wall studs on the left side of the room while Bridges took the right. And found nothing. The area beneath the stairs revealed the same.

Nothing.

They devoured the coffee and pastries before moving down to the basement. The lanterns they'd used most of the night had been exchanged for a couple that still held the better portion of their kerosene. Camille had located a sledgehammer and traded it with Bridges for the smaller hammer she'd been using before.

Like most all New England homes, Beacon Manor had an extensive basement. Generally the heating oil tanks were found there as well as the old furnaces and lots of stored goods. Mostly junk.

The basement was divided into three sections. The larger main section that was original to the house, then two side sections that had been added later. The dank, musty smell was matched by the stench of old heating oil. The lanterns struggled against the thick darkness but managed to provide fairly decent illumination. Enough to do what had to be done.

"I've already searched the boxes and shelves." Nicholas indicated the pieces of stored furniture and the items stacked near or atop them. There really wasn't anyplace else to search. "About all we can look for here is some sort of hidden room or tunnel." He locked gazes with Bridges. "I've never known there to be either but we can check it out just to be sure."

"Sounds like a plan." Bridges set his sledgehammer aside and, with Camille holding the lantern at just the right level, he began inspecting the rock walls.

Something like jealousy had Nicholas breathing as if he'd run a marathon. What was wrong with him? The two were still involved, obviously. He had no right to begrudge whatever happiness they found together.

Nicholas turned to the opposite wall with his lantern. He placed his hand on the cool stone and started the arduous, time-consuming task. The walls were naturally uneven. The stones of varying sizes and chinked together with crumbling mortar. If there was an irregularity it might not be easy to spot.

Slowly, methodically, he searched a section at a time. The silence was broken only by the occasional shuffle of feet. There was nothing to say. This was their last hope and no one wanted to admit that this whole night may have been wasted on a dead end.

The silly riddles and rhymes his grandfather had singsonged every day of Nicholas's life played over and over in his head, taunting him. What the hell did any of it mean? Could it be that this entire effort was futile? That the curse was nothing but a stupid legend? Had Nicholas begun to obsess about the curse because his whole life had gone to hell after the fire?

No. He stilled. He'd heard that voice…had felt the certainty that night when his grandfather died. The curse was real. Restoring the lighthouse and lantern was Raven's Cliff's only hope. It was *his* only hope.

Finding the lens could very well be Camille's only chance of getting her child back.

His child.

"Find something?"

Nicholas whipped around at the sound of Bridges's voice. He tamped down the fury that instantly mounted at seeing the man huddled near the other wall with Camille at his side. He had no right, he reminded himself. "Not yet. You?"

Bridges shook his head and got back to his task. Camille never looked up.

Just as well. The last thing Nicholas wanted her to see was anything resembling jealously in his eyes or on his face.

He turned back to the wall, but something made him hesitate.

Nicholas frowned.

What was that sound?

It came again. A distant thump, thump, thump.

"Did you hear that?" Camille asked.

Nicholas listened again. "I think someone's at the door." He headed for the steps. "I'll check it out."

He didn't look back but he assumed that Camille and Bridges carried on with their search. Nicholas didn't want to look. He might catch Bridges in the act of stealing a kiss or touching Camille in some way that...

That nothing.

Camille didn't belong to Nicholas.

He stormed through the entry hall just as another round of banging echoed from the front door. He didn't bother asking who was there when he probably should have. Instead he jerked the door open and glared.

Chief Swanson.

"Sterling, good." The chief rubbed his knuckles as if they still stung from rapping on the door. "I was beginning to think no one was here." He glanced at the two vehicles sitting in front of the house.

"What can I do for you, Chief?" Nicholas was busy. He had no desire to stand around chatting. If the chief had news he should get to it. If he came just to check up on Nicholas he should leave now.

"We don't have anything new on the missing Wells baby. I checked in with the Bureau right before I drove over here. There's no news at all unless the P.I. Perry hired has found something." The chief held a small plastic bag up where Nicholas could see. "But we did find this near the rubble of your cottage. I was wondering if you recognized it."

Nicholas took the bag and stared at the object inside. A silver ring with a five-point star encased in a circle. A pentagram? An image flashed in his mind, but it was too swift and fleeting for him to make it out. He stared a moment longer at the ring, but nothing clicked. Shaking his head, he handed it back to the chief. "It doesn't belong to me."

"Lagios says it looks like one your dead twin brother wore."

The frown already plaguing Nicholas's brow deepened. "Alex?" Nicholas couldn't say for sure. He'd never noticed any jewelry but then they hadn't actually interacted until right before Alex's death. "I don't know. Perhaps." Alex had been the Seaside Strangler. He'd plunged over the cliffs to his death while attempting to sacrifice another victim. Nicholas had witnessed his twin's fatal plunge. "What difference does it make? He's dead."

The chief shrugged noncommittally. "I don't know. But, like I said, we found this near the cottage. I guess I'm just wondering how it might have gotten there seeing as the last we saw of Gibson he was taking a swan dive over the cliffs and Lagios is convinced he was wearing this ring when he died."

"That's possible I guess, but, like I said, he's dead," Nicholas repeated.

"Is he?" Swanson studied Nicholas. "His body wasn't found, which isn't all that unusual considering the current. But then again, we thought you were dead for five years. And we both know Camille survived a similar fall."

Could Alex still be alive? Was he the man Nicholas saw in his vision with Camille's child?

Fear banded around Nicholas's chest.

His brother had probably remembered the caves where they had played as children. He had likely studied the rhymes and artwork the two of them had made there. Had seeing those images or reading those words made him remember something their grandfather had said before Alex was sent away?

If Alex was alive and *if* he had Camille's child…the chances of a safe recovery were slim to none.

Alex was insane.

And if he survived that plunge…he would be out for vengeance.

Chapter Eleven

Camille reached the entry hall just as Nicholas closed the door. She'd left Grant in the basement. She'd excused herself by saying she needed to find someplace to relieve herself. Which was true, but she'd really wanted a moment alone with Nicholas. Or did she just need some space? As much as she appreciated all Grant was doing and his seemingly endless well of forgiveness, he was beginning to get on her nerves. He was being *too* good. It felt…strange. But maybe she was tired and overreacting.

"Who was that?" she asked as he turned from the door.

"The chief." His expression was carefully guarded, which set her immediately on edge.

"Did he have news?" Her heart reacted to

the possibility. Why hadn't someone called her? She instinctively pulled her cell phone from her pocket to check the battery. Still had a partial charge. Her gaze connected with Nicholas's once more.

"No. No news."

When he started to walk past her to go back to the basement she laid a hand on his arm. "I didn't mean for…" How did she say this? He paused, but didn't look at her. "I shouldn't have pushed you to kiss me. I was feeling vulnerable and afraid."

And stupid.

She'd promised herself she would never fall for Nicholas again. But she was vulnerable right now. She'd let the moment get out of control. That couldn't happen again.

"No problem."

He walked away, left her there to wallow in her guilt.

Obviously he hadn't been affected by the moment. Why had she been?

Why was she still?

Because she was a fool.

A fool whose child was missing.

Camille closed her eyes and covered her face

with her hands. She had to pull herself together and focus. They had about twenty-four hours left. If they didn't find the lens soon…

They would find it.

They had to find it.

She dropped her hands to her sides, lifted her chin and reached down deep for her determination. Stay on track.

Nothing mattered but baby Nigel.

Her son.

Camille took a breath and headed for the back door leading to the yard. With no power, the well couldn't pump water. With no water, she couldn't use the bathroom in the house. After she'd found a private spot in back of the house to relieve herself, she hurried back to the basement. As she descended the stairs she was struck by the tension in the air.

Had something happened in the few moments she'd been gone?

Nicholas and Grant were huddled in one corner, their voices low.

Anticipation zipped along her nerve endings.

"Did you find something?"

"Bring your lantern!" Nicholas shouted over his shoulder.

Grant glanced up at her as she neared, lantern held high. The look lasted only a moment, but there was a ferocity about it that startled her.

"What'd you find?" A mixture of worry and hope swirled inside her. Maybe he'd picked up on her impatience with him.

Nicholas traced a path in the mortar space between the rocks. "There's a sizable gap here where the mortar is missing entirely."

"Did the mortar deteriorate?" She'd noticed several places where the mortar had crumbled away. But surely Nicholas had noticed, as well. This had to be more than that, or the two wouldn't be so excited.

He shook his head. "I don't think there was ever any in this space."

"We think," Grant added, meeting her gaze again, only this time with something like anticipation in his eyes, "a section of the wall may slide inward."

Camille used her lantern to follow the empty mortar space around a large section of stone. Grant was right. It did appear to outline an area big enough for a door of sorts. But how did it open?

"Use the lantern to watch the space on this side." Nicholas gestured to the space to his left. "Let us know if it changes in depth or width."

Now she understood why they had wanted her lantern close by. The one Nicholas had been using was burning dimly now. The kerosene was just about gone from the base.

"Gotcha." Camille held the lantern at the best position for watching the line between the rocks. "I'm ready."

Grunting with the effort, Nicholas and Grant pushed against the section of rock wall. As hard and long as they heaved, nothing happened.

Frustration unfurled in her belly. "Maybe there's a catch or latch somewhere close by." She surveyed the area, looking for anything that protruded or appeared different from the rest of the wall.

"We've already looked," Grant explained. "We didn't find anything."

Camille backed up a step and studied the floor, then overhead. There had to be something.

"Let's give it another go," Nicholas said to Grant.

As Camille stepped forward to watch the empty mortar space once more, something on the edge of her vision snagged her attention. She scanned the place where the rock wall met the wooden ceiling. The ceiling was made up of tongue-and-groove boards, but two in particular held her attention. There was a wider gap on either side of those two than between any of the others.

"What's this?" She pointed to the spot. It could be nothing, but then again it could be significant.

Grant was the one to reach up first. Since the ceiling was slightly lower than the traditional eight feet, he easily reached the boards in question. He pushed against them with his fingers, but nothing happened. The boards didn't move, nor did anything else.

Nicholas looked from the boards to the wall, then he reached up and pressed against the two boards where they met the wall.

The boards gave way. A click echoed beyond the rock wall. The section of wall sank inward just an inch, maybe two.

Camille gasped. Her pulse jumped. They'd found it. A secret passage!

Grant started to push on the wall again, but Nicholas held up a hand. "Let me go first."

Grant obliged by stepping back. Camille's body began to tremble with anticipation.

Please, please, let this be it. Let them find the lens and rescue my baby.

Nicholas leaned his full body weight against the section of wall and it moved inward another inch, then another. He pushed harder, and suddenly it moved all the way inward.

Any oxygen left in Camille's lungs evacuated. Her heart thundered so hard she couldn't hope to regain her breath.

Nicholas took the lantern from her shaky fingers and, with one final look at her, entered the passageway.

Grant started to follow him, but hesitated to allow Camille to go first.

The smell of moss and dampness invaded her lungs with a gulp of air. The passageway reminded her of the caves. Dark and damp… cold. To her left, behind the opening, was a dead end.

"This way." Nicholas motioned for them to follow as he continued along the passage in the other direction.

It wasn't as narrow as she'd expected. The farther from the entrance they moved, the wider the passage—three or three and a half feet.

They rounded a corner and the passage spilled into a sizable room. In the middle of the room was a wood table. A lantern sat on the table. Nicholas withdrew the matches from his pocket and lit the lamp. Incredibly there was ample kerosene in its base.

Nicholas wiped the dust from the table to reveal words written on the surface.

Behind the loosened stones lies the treasure you seek.

Camille turned around slowly, shone the light of her lantern on the stone walls. Where? Good Lord! Where? The loose stones had to be in this room! She was so sick of these crazy riddles.

"Here!" Grant rushed to the far side of the room and placed his hand on the wall. "These are loose."

Nicholas and Camille joined him. He was right. The stones were dry stacked, not mortared.

Reaching for the first one, Nicholas said, "Let's put them on the floor in the exact order we take them out."

She didn't know what difference that made, but she did as he said. With her lantern on the floor, she and Grant took the stones Nicholas removed and placed them in order next to the lantern.

When the last one was removed, Nicholas stared into the opening.

Camille held her breath, prayed this was it.

Nicholas reached inside and dragged a large wooden crate to the edge of the opening. He turned to Grant. "I'm going to need your help."

Grant got into position and the two hefted the crate from the hole in the wall and carried it to the table. Camille couldn't get oxygen into her lungs fast enough. This was it. She could feel it. The air crackled with anticipation. The others had to feel it, too.

"We're going to need the hammer," Nicholas said.

"I'll get it." Grant hustled back in the direction of the basement.

Camille dared to approach the crate then. "Do you think this is it?"

Nicholas nodded. He didn't know how to articulate the feeling, but he could sense that the crate contained the lens. His instincts were humming.

Pain abruptly seared through his brain. He closed his eyes and held still a moment to ride it out. But it wasn't going away so easily. He could hear Camille asking him if he was all right, but he couldn't answer. A vision filled his head. The images were blurry at first, but then they cleared. Rock walls…the musty smell. He was back in the passage…no, no, not this passage. The other place with its white corridors. But he wasn't in the corridors. He was beneath the corridors where the walls were stone like here in this room. He could hear crying… frantic, wailing.

The baby.

His son.

His chest seized with an emotion he couldn't name.

He followed the sound, his heart pounding harder and harder, threatening to burst from his chest.

And then he found the child. Still in the

cradle. Tiny arms and legs flailing with frustration.

The baby was hungry.

"Nicholas!"

He jerked with another blast of pain. Then the images faded, leaving him weak and unsteady on his feet.

"Nicholas, are you all right?"

"I'm fine," he grunted. He had to hurry. If his insane brother had left the baby unattended and unfed... Nicholas had to hurry.

"Is everything all right?" Bridges joined them at the table, the hammer in his hand.

Nicholas didn't answer. He reached for the hammer and began the careful process of opening the container.

Camille and Bridges watched quietly while Nicholas loosened the top of the crate with the claw of the hammer. When he'd succeeded in pulling free all the nails, he set the hammer aside and took a moment to steady his trembling hands.

On some level he still didn't like it that Bridges was a part of this, but it was too late to worry about that now. He was here.

"Can I do it?"

His gaze collided with Camille's. The hope combined with lingering fear he saw in her eyes made the decision for him. He stepped aside and let her lift the lid from the crate.

Straw was packed around whatever was inside. She reached inside and moved the straw two handfuls at a time. That was when they got their first glimpse of the glittering stones.

"Oh…my God," she whispered. "This is it."

Nicholas reached inside with both hands and lifted the heavy lens from the container. Bridges quickly grabbed the container and set it aside on the floor. Nicholas slowly lowered the lens to the table.

"It's beautiful."

He turned to Camille. "It is."

Larger than a basketball, but incredibly small compared to the power it radiated, the diamond-shaped lens glittered in the dim light, reflecting and magnifying even the faint flow of the lantern.

"There's a stone missing," Bridges said, his voice thick with his own awe.

Nicholas leaned in that direction and noted that Bridges was correct. One stone was missing. He moved around Bridges and knelt next to the crate. Nicholas dug around in the straw at the bottom. His fingers closed around something smooth and warm. A stone. His fingers brushed another and then another after that. He placed each on the table.

The stones on the lens looked crystal clear and glittered like diamonds. But the ones he'd found loose in the crate were colored. One red, one blue and one purple. That couldn't be right.

"Which one fills that void?" Bridges asked, looking from the stones to the empty spot on the lens.

The worry was back on Camille's face. "Does it matter? Can't we just give it to him like this?"

She didn't have to say the rest. She wanted her baby back now.

Nicholas thought about that a moment and decided she was right. It wasn't as if the bastard was going to have time to figure it out. Nicholas wasn't letting this lens out of his sight. He would get the baby, but no one was escaping with the lens. "He asked for the lens. This is it."

When Nicholas reached for the crate,

Bridges picked up the lid he had removed. "Wait," he said. "There's something written here."

Nicholas moved closer to him and read the words seemingly branded into the underside of the wooden lid.

Only he who has been selected can choose the stone...red, blue or purple. The wrong choice and the rest darken and die.

"That has to mean you," Bridges said, his eyes oddly wide, almost wild.

"I suppose it is." Nicholas shrugged. "But that's not my problem right now." He picked up the crate. "It's his." If Alex was behind this, Nicholas would make sure he was dead this time. And then Nicholas would figure out the puzzle of the stones. He wasn't giving the enemy any help.

"No."

Nicholas turned to Bridges. What the hell was wrong with him?

"Grant?" Camille moved closer to Nicholas. "Are you okay?"

"Of course I'm not okay," he snarled. He

bent down and snagged a small pistol from what appeared to be an ankle holster.

Nicholas stepped slightly in front of Camille. "What is this, Bridges?"

The man who'd stood up for him against the villagers? Who'd helped them search and brought coffee...now held a gun in his hand?

"The lens is mine," he lashed out at Nicholas. "It was stolen from my family."

Of all the tales Nicholas had heard about the lens and the lighthouse, he'd never heard that one. "Can you prove that accusation?" Remaining calm and rational would be best for now. Bridges was clearly suffering from some kind of delusion. Maybe it was the lens. Nicholas's grandfather had always said it held some sort of mystical powers. In the wrong hands it could be dangerous.

Right now they needed to make the man holding Camille's baby believe he was going to get it. They didn't have time to waste on Bridges now that his motive for being so helpful was revealed. Nicholas should never have told him about the lens after the kidnapper's call.

"My great-great-great-great—" Bridges

smirked "—you get the picture. My ancestor designed both the lenses. Then he was cheated out of his share."

Nicholas did get the picture. Had Bridges ever been his true friend? Apparently not. "And what was his share?"

Bridges pointed the gun at the lens. "One should have been his."

"But," Nicholas argued cautiously, "your ancestor was commissioned to design these for use in the lighthouse. I'm sure he was paid for his work."

"It wasn't nearly enough," Bridges snarled, edged closer with the gun trained on Nicholas's heart. "My family has spent generations looking for this damned lens. All this time we foolishly thought the old bastard had hidden it away on one of the islands. That's what he claimed." Bridges shook his head. "We've searched and searched and searched. All the time it was right here under our noses." Bridges huffed. "I've crawled through the caves and passageways around this stupid lighthouse." He waved the gun madly. "Do you realize that this is the only one I couldn't find?"

Nicholas gestured to the lens. "We can deal with your issues after we get the baby back." Surely if the man had any feelings for Camille he would listen to reason.

Bridges's gaze was glued to the lens. "I want it now."

"But what about the man who has my baby?" Camille cried. "You can't take it, Grant."

"She's right, Bridges," Nicholas reminded him. A new kind of tension was building in him now. He had a very bad feeling about this.

Bridges laughed long and loud. "Please, Camille, that damned brat has driven me crazy for weeks. I can't wait to be rid of the little bastard."

Camille swayed. Nicholas grabbed her just in time before her knees gave way.

"You have my son?" Her voice was scarcely a whisper.

"Of course." Bridges grinned. "Don't you remember anything?" He laughed again. "That idiot Alex had fished you out of the water and kept you alive in case he needed to manipulate the mayor. I'd been watching him. Following him to and from the inn. I knew what he was up to. When I followed him to your hiding place, I stole you away from him. Waited for you to have the baby and, well—" he shrugged "—you know the rest." He looked at Nicholas then. "And just so you know, he's dead. I combed the shore until his body washed up. I borrowed the ring just to bug the chief, then sent dear old Alex out to sea."

Fury claimed Camille. "You left me for dead, you son of a bitch."

Nicholas tightened his hold on her waist for fear she would make a dive for Bridges, gun or no gun.

"I had a plan." Grant's grin widened. "I knew if you were all helpless and pathetic that Sterling here would do whatever was necessary to help you. And here we are."

"But we were getting married," she said, some of the fight draining out of her tone.

Nicholas wanted to hear the answer to this, but even more important, he wanted to figure out a way to overcome Bridges. Once Camille was safe, he planned to beat the hell out of the guy before calling the chief.

"Yes, we were. As long as I was connected

to you I would be connected to him." He jerked his head toward Nicholas. "But when you told me about the baby, I realized I had the perfect opportunity to get what I wanted a whole lot faster." He looked at Nicholas. "I was really tired of waiting for you to get the courage to claim what was rightfully yours and begin your restoration." He snickered. "I knew you wouldn't be able to resist, that the curse would draw you back here if you were still alive and you'd make it your quest to find the lens. Guilt is such a great motivator."

"Where's my son?" Camille demanded, trying to make that dive Nicholas had expected. He held her back.

"When your lover here selects the proper stone, I'll walk out of here with the lens. Then, when I'm well out of reach, I'll call you with the location of the little brat and we'll all live happily ever after." He shook his head. "If I'd known he could work this fast I would've given you twenty-four hours instead of forty-eight." He lifted an eyebrow in disdain. "Just to make it interesting."

"You sick bastard." Camille made another of those lunges for him.

"Camille," Nicholas murmured against her hair as he held her firmly against him. "This is not the way."

She jerked at his hold once, then twice before surrendering to his strength.

"Do it," Bridges ordered. With the gun he gestured to the lens.

Nicholas looked Camille straight in the eyes. "If I let you go, you promise me you won't do anything stupid?"

For one moment he wasn't sure she would agree, then she nodded. Nicholas had a plan. When Bridges reached for the lens he would need both hands. Nicholas would overwhelm him then.

"Okay." Nicholas released her. She backed away a step, glared at Bridges, but made no move to attack him.

"Hurry up, Sterling. That squalling brat is probably hungry."

Nicholas blinked, thought of the vision he'd had. Yes, his son was hungry. His lips flattened. Bridges would pay for this.

"So which one is it?" Bridges demanded.

Nicholas looked at the three stones. He had no idea which was the right one. But he had to make a choice. He reached for the purple one. The color of power. That made sense.

As soon as his fingers curled around the stone, a brilliant light shot through his brain. He froze. Couldn't even breathe.

Choose carefully, boy. The wrong choice will end your life and destroy Raven's Cliff. Salvation lies inside you and you alone. Nicholas shuddered with the overwhelming emotions that accompanied his grandfather's voice reverberating in his brain. He wanted to cry. Wanted to beg for forgiveness. *Now is not the time, boy,* his grandfather whispered in a gentle voice that only Nicholas could hear. *There is only one way to make the past right and that will come later. Now you must make the correct choice. I think you know that the choice is not about power…it's about heart.*

"What are you waiting for, Sterling?" Bridges demanded.

Nicholas stared at the purple stone in his hand. He let go a ragged breath. "This is the right stone." He held it out to Bridges. "But if the lens is yours, then you must be the one to position it in its rightful place."

Camille looked from Nicholas to Bridges and back, fear screaming in her eyes.

Nicholas pointed a "trust me" glance in her direction. "It's the right thing to do."

"Give me the stone." Bridges snatched the stone from Nicholas's hand. "Don't get any ideas. Back off." He motioned with the gun, urging them to step away from the table.

Nicholas dragged Camille back a few steps with him. She resisted at first, but then relented.

She shook her head as Bridges worked to lodge the stone into place. "How could he do this?" she muttered.

Nicholas couldn't answer the question. But he understood that greed could be a powerful motivator.

"Aha!" Bridges dropped his hand away from the lens, the purple stone in place. "That's it." He aimed the gun at Nicholas. "Now to finish this."

"No!" Camille screamed.

Before Bridges could pull the trigger the lens started to vibrate.

"What the hell?" he muttered as his attention shifted from Nicholas and Camille to the lens.

The vibration grew louder and then the

light seemed to explode from the lens, quickly getting brighter.

Nicholas wrapped his arms around Camille and held her protectively against his chest.

"This is amazing!" Bridges screamed.

At that precise instant a beam of light shot from the lens and pierced the bastard's chest like a laser.

The gun fell from his limp fingers as the light receded back into the lens.

Bridges bumped the table as he fell forward. The red stone slid off the edge of the table.

"No!" Nicholas dove for the stone. He barely caught it before it shattered on the floor.

For three beats Nicholas could only lie there cradling the precious stone.

Finally, when Camille's voice got through to him, he scrambled to his feet.

"Are you okay?" She looked him over as if fearing the light had pierced him as it had Bridges.

He nodded. "I'm okay. But the stone." He exhaled a breath. "We almost lost it."

"Are you sure it's the right one?" She looked at the blue one still lying on the table. "It could be the blue one."

Nicholas shook his head. "No. It's the red one."

He removed the now ugly, dark purple stone. Apparently the power from the lens had turned it black. Saying a final prayer that his instincts were right, he tucked the red stone into position.

The vibration started again. Light glittered and brightened from the lens.

"Nicholas!" Camille threw her arms around him and held him as if she thought her body would somehow protect him.

He held her as the light filled the room, even brighter than before. In those moments before it faded, he saw Raven's Cliff's future. Nicholas smiled. Finally he would be able to right his mistakes.

After carefully repacking the lens in its container and returning it to the hiding place that had protected it for centuries, Nicholas dragged Bridges's body back into the basement. He secured the entry to the passageway, and he and Camille ascended to the first floor.

Nicholas called the chief to advise him of what had happened. They didn't have to worry about Alex Gibson. He was dead. Grant Bridges was the man responsible for the latest trouble.

When he'd closed the phone, Camille searched his face. "What do we do now? My baby is still missing. Grant's dead. What if we can't find where he was keeping him before it's…too late?"

Nicholas pulled her into his arms and held her tighter than he had ever held her before. "Don't worry." Determination solidified inside him. "I will find your baby."

Chapter Twelve

Camille paced the floor of the chief's office. She couldn't stop wringing her hands. Grant had been dead for two hours and they hadn't figured out where to look for her baby. They had searched his room at the inn, his car, his person. And found nothing.

Fear coiled inside her, making her body tremble even harder. What if they were too late?

Nicholas stood by quietly. He had discussed his visions with the chief. They were attempting to determine a location based on what little he could recall from the blurry visions.

But it was so little detail.

And Nicholas himself had said the baby was crying in his vision. Oh, God. What was she going to do? How much longer was this going to take?

"Sterling." The chief stormed into his office, one of his deputies on his heels. "Officer Smith here thinks he might know what it is you've been seeing in those visions of yours."

Camille held her breath, sent one final prayer heavenward.

The cop nodded at her, then at Nicholas. "Sounds to me like you're describing the old monastery."

"The monastery?" Nicholas echoed.

Smith nodded again. "During the outbreak related to those poison fish, the doctors set up a secure clinic in the monastery. Before it was over we discovered some passages in the walls that went underground." Another of those nods sent his head jerking up and down. "And those corridors over there are white, just like you saw in your…your, ah, vision."

"Let's go." Nicholas grabbed Camille's hand and headed for the door.

"You can ride with me," the chief said to Nicholas and Camille. "Smith, you grab a couple other men and meet us over there in case we run into any trouble."

Camille could hardly breathe as they made the trip to the edge of town and the monastery that had stood there for as long as she could remember. The trees crowded in on the road and scarcely opened to allow entrance to the abandoned property. Her chest felt tight, and her heart floundered behind her sternum. She should have called her parents. But she hadn't thought of anything except her child.

What if he wasn't here?

She surveyed the woods around the abandoned monastery. A high fence surrounded the property. It looked like a prison or an institution. It was no place for a sweet, innocent baby.

One of the chief's men jumped out and opened the gate. Once it was open, they drove through and onto the property. Three stories of stone towered before her. Camille had never been inside the building, that she remembered. God only knew where she'd been kept during those missing months. Covered with moss and ivy, the monastery looked as ominous as she'd always envisioned.

The chief fumbled with a ring of keys until he found the right one to open the door. Once inside, the men would spread out and begin a methodical search of the building.

The door had no sooner swung inward than the chief held up a hand. "Nobody move."

Fear surged inside Camille. She wanted desperately to know what the chief had found, but like everyone else, she stood frozen by his command. It was impossible to see beyond him, but something had definitely stopped him.

Chief Swanson crouched just inside the doorway. A few trauma-filled moments later, he stood and turned back to the crowd. His gaze settled on Camille. "We've got a body inside…"

Her heart stalled in her chest.

"But it's not your baby. It's Albert Syler."

Relief rushed through Camille, sending her heart pounding again. "Who's Albert Syler?"

"A fisherman who moved here a couple of years ago. Sort of a loner. My guess is he was working for Bridges." The chief's worried gaze rested fully on Camille once more. "There's a baby bottle lying on the floor next to his body. Bridges must've decided he didn't want any loose ends."

That meant her baby was in there!

The full reality of what Grant had done hit

Camille then. He'd never intended to tell her where her baby was. He would have killed both Nicholas and her and left her baby *here* to die…alone.

Dear God, how could he have pretended to care? How could she…the whole village, for that matter…have misjudged him so?

"Listen up," the chief said then. "We need to get this search started. The state police can deal with the body and the scene. We're going inside and start the search. There's no time to waste. But I don't want anyone going near the body. No matter that this is likely Bridges's doing, it's still a crime scene and should be treated as such."

The chief opened the door wide and stepped aside. His deputies had filed in around Camille before she gathered her wits and moved inside, as well. Nicholas didn't wait for her. She was thankful. Someone had to pull it together enough to do what needed to be done. Clearly it wasn't her.

She stepped inside, giving the motionless body on the floor a wide berth. She didn't look at the man she hadn't known. Couldn't feel any sympathy for him. He had helped hide her baby.

Still, before she moved completely away she paused. Couldn't help herself. She had to look back. Not at the body, but at the bottle. Her baby's bottle.

Fury boiled up inside her. She would find her baby.

Camille wandered the corridors, tears gliding down her cheeks as she listened to the pounding of footsteps. Every time the "clear" signal was called, her heart dropped lower and lower in her chest.

They had to find him. Camille couldn't stand it any longer. She ran from wing to wing until she found Nicholas. "Have you found the underground passage yet?"

He shook his head. "No one seems to recall precisely where the access is. The chief's got a call in to the doc over at the clinic to see if she recalls. Those are bad memories. Folks have put a lot behind them."

Camille wanted to scream. She wanted to run through the corridors calling her baby's name.

"Shh."

She turned to Nicholas.

Those piercing blue eyes bored into hers. "Close your eyes and picture your baby."

She made one of those little sobbing sounds. "I can't even remember seeing my baby."

Nicholas passed his fingertips over her lids to usher them down. "He has dark hair."

Camille's lips quivered.

"He's strong and he wants his mother."

Please, she prayed, *let me find him!* A man was dead—Grant had likely killed him. Had he killed her baby? God, she couldn't believe that—she had to have faith. They had to find her child. She had to believe they would. Nicholas believed the baby was there, according to his visions.

Nicholas pressed his forehead to hers. "He's going to be an artist. He has long fingers."

Camille held Nicholas's hands. "Tell me more," she whispered.

Nicholas squeezed his eyes shut and summoned the visions he usually struggled to keep at bay. He didn't like it when he saw things. It didn't happen often, especially not since Alex had died. But now he needed to see.

He concentrated with all his might.

Searched his brain for the memories of the other two visions.

The pain seared through his head. He shuddered with the force of it.

He could hear the baby crying. Could see his little arms and legs swinging with anger and frustration.

In this new vision, Nicholas turned away from the cradle and walked down the dark passage. He moved and moved and moved until he found the narrow rock stairs.

Up, he commanded himself. *Go up the stairs.*

In the vision he moved up the stairs, slowly, so damned slowly.

He reached an opening. Walked through. The walls were white now. He moved through a small white room and into the corridor.

Look around, he ordered.

In the vision, he stopped and looked around the corridor.

Nicholas straightened. Opened his eyes. Camille stared at him, her eyes full of hope. He tightened his hold on her hand. "This way."

He all but ran along the corridor until he found the intersecting one he wanted. "This way." He rushed toward the door he remembered vividly from the vision.

Once in the small room, he released Camille's hand. "The entry to the passage is somewhere in here."

They searched the walls and floor until they were both ready to give up.

Then Nicholas found it. A column that seemed formed in the wall. A decorative accent with a hidden purpose, a kind of raised molding. He moved his hand over it, around it. *There.* He touched a small section that protruded slightly. The entryway moved inward. As soon as the stones were separated, the sound of wailing echoed through.

"My baby!"

Nicholas held Camille's hand as they descended the narrow twisting staircase. They rushed along the passageway until they found the cradle...and the baby.

Camille could scarcely see for the tears as she reached for her baby. She held him close. She'd been right—a boy. His little body stiffened as he screamed bloody murder.

She quickly checked him for injury. He wailed insistently through her every touch.

"We should get him to the clinic," Nicholas suggested.

Camille nodded. "Thank you." Her lips trembled. "I might never have found him without your help."

Nicholas nodded. "It was the least I could do."

Camille held the baby out to him. "Will you carry your son up the stairs?"

He hesitated. Wasn't sure he could or should…

And then his son was in his arms. The emotions that bombarded him would not be limited by mere words.

Peace filled Nicholas for the first time in many, many years.

Everything was going to be fine. Raven's Cliff was going to be fine.

And so was Camille. And he.

And their son.

Epilogue

Nine months later...

Nicholas set the paint roller aside and wiped his damp brow. He was almost finished with the interior painting of his home.

He considered all that he had done in the past few months. The lighthouse was fully restored. The house was nearing completion. Other than the rest of this damned painting. And a few other odds and ends.

"Nicholas!"

His lips stretched into a smile as Camille strode through the open front door, little Nigel on her hip.

"Hey." Nicholas kissed her on the cheek and then kissed the top of his son's head.

Nigel Earl. Earl after the old sea captain. It was only fitting.

"My, you're sweaty, Mr. Sterling."

Nicholas reached for his water bottle and took a long swig. "That's because I'm working hard, Mrs. Sterling."

He and Camille had gotten married four months ago. Her parents had accepted the marriage, had even apologized to both Camille and Nicholas. No one in the village could believe what Bridges had done. The villagers hadn't openly apologized to Nicholas, but they had accepted him, and that was enough. Camille had helped him with the work on the house after he'd completed the lighthouse restoration. Between helping him and taking care of their son, she had been a busy lady. As her mind had healed from the stress, she'd slowly regained most of her memory. There were some things they might never know, but they had each other and together they would get through whatever came their way.

"The mayor called," she said as she allowed Nigel's feet to touch the floor. She held both his hands and helped him walk. He was so close. He'd be walking on his own any day now.

"And what did the mayor have to say?" Even Simpson had come around where Nicholas was concerned. Simpson was actually doing amazing things for the village. The fishing industry was at an all-time high. Several small businesses had moved in, along with a couple of fancy restaurants. The village was booming.

"He wants to know if the celebration committee can get started on the decorating two hours early." Camille's blue eyes glittered with pride as she gazed into Nicholas's.

She was proud of him. He'd done all the right things, and there wasn't a soul in the village who considered him a beast anymore. More important, he had proved how much he loved her, and she had done the same.

Tonight the entire village would gather at the lighthouse to celebrate its lighting for the first time in six years. Tonight was the night. Tonight Nicholas would be able to do what he had failed to do six years ago.

"You know—" Camille hefted their baby in her arms and sashayed closer to Nicholas "—Nigel's really tired. If he goes down for his nap early…and we get in the shower…"

Nicholas kissed her sweet lips. "Now, that is my kind of celebration."

As Camille had predicted, the baby took an early nap. She and Nicholas were able to hold a private celebration of their own… that included a shower and crisp white bedsheets with candles all around the room. Then later wine and cheese and grapes and more lovemaking.

That evening, as the sun set and after the crowd had gathered, Nicholas, with his son in one arm, lit the lantern just as the old sea captain had ordered so very long ago.

When he climbed back down the stairs he found his wife, and together they watched the waves roll in to shore. The ocean was endless and ferocious, yet the sound lulled their son to sleep each night.

Nicholas blinked, rubbed at his eyes. Was he seeing things?

He started to ask Camille if she saw it, too, but she was busy laughing with the baby, so he didn't. Maybe Nicholas had had too much wine, but he was certain he could see a small rowboat with four people inside. One looked exactly like the captain. The captain figure leaned slightly to the side and executed a sharp salute.

Nicholas smiled. Had that salute been for him? He glanced around at the other folks gathered. Did no one see this but him?

When Nicholas stared back out to sea, all he saw were the waves. The captain and his family were gone. At peace at last.

That was the way Nicholas would keep it, too. Every year at this time he would do his duty. He looked down at his son. And years from now his son would, as well.

They were the keepers of the lighthouse.

And Raven's Cliff would forever prosper under their caring watch.

* * * * *

Here's a sneak peek at
THE CEO'S CHRISTMAS PROPOSITION,
the first in USA TODAY *bestselling author*
Merline Lovelace's HOLIDAYS ABROAD
trilogy coming in November 2008.

American Devon McShay is about to get
the Christmas surprise of a lifetime when
she meets her new client, sexy billionaire
Caleb Logan, for the very first time.

Silhouette®

Desire

Available November 2008

Her breath whistled out in a sigh of relief when he exited Customs. Devon recognized him right away from the newspaper and magazine articles her friend and partner Sabrina had looked up during her frantic prep work.

Caleb John Logan, Jr. Thirty-one. Six-two. With jet-black hair, laser-blue eyes and a linebacker's shoulders under his charcoal-gray cashmere overcoat. His jaw-dropping good looks didn't score him any points with

Devon. She'd learned the hard way not to trust handsome heartbreakers like Cal Logan.

But he was a client. An important one. And she was willing to give someone who'd served a hitch in the marines before earning a B.S. from the University of Oregon, an MBA from Stanford and his first million at the ripe old age of twenty-six the benefit of the doubt.

Right up until he spotted the hot-pink pashmina, that is.

Devon knew the flash of color was more visible than the sign she held up with his name on it. So she wasn't surprised when Logan picked her out of the crowd and cut in her direction. She'd just plastered on her best businesswoman smile when he whipped an arm around her waist. The next moment she was sprawled against his cashmere-covered chest.

"Hello, brown eyes."

Swooping down, he covered her mouth with his.

Sheer astonishment kept Devon rooted to the spot for a few seconds while her mind whirled chaotically. Her first thought was that her client had downed a few too many drinks during the long flight. Her second, that he'd mistaken the kind of escort and consulting services her company provided. Her third shoved everything else out of her head.

The man could kiss!

His mouth moved over hers with a skill that ignited sparks at a half dozen flash points throughout her body. Devon hadn't experienced that kind of spontaneous combustion in a while. A *long* while.

The sparks were still popping when she pushed off his chest, only now they fueled a flush of anger.

"Do you always greet women you don't know with a lip-lock, Mr. Logan?"

A smile crinkled the skin at the corners of his eyes. "As a matter of fact, I don't. That was from Don."

"Huh?"

"He said he owed you one from New Year's Eve two years ago and made me promise to deliver it."

She stared up at him in total incomprehension. Logan hooked a brow and attempted to prompt a nonexistent memory.

"He abandoned you at the Waldorf. Five minutes before midnight. To deliver twins."

"I don't have a clue who or what you're…"

Understanding burst like a water balloon.

"Wait a sec. Are you talking about Sabrina's old boyfriend? Your buddy, who's now an ob-gyn doc?"

It was Logan's turn to look startled. He recovered faster than Devon had, though. His smile widened into a rueful grin.

"I take it you're not Sabrina Russo."

"No, Mr. Logan, I am *not*."

* * * * *

Be sure to look for
THE CEO'S CHRISTMAS PROPOSITION
by Merline Lovelace.
Available in November 2008
wherever books are sold, including
most bookstores, supermarkets,
drugstores and discount stores.

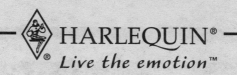

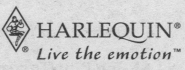

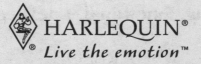

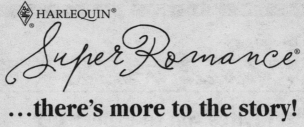

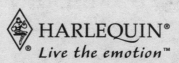

HARLEQUIN®
Presents

The world's bestselling romance series...
The series that brings you your favorite authors,
month after month:

Helen Bianchin...Emma Darcy
Lynne Graham...Penny Jordan
Miranda Lee...Sandra Marton
Anne Mather...Carole Mortimer
Melanie Milburne...Michelle Reid

and many more talented authors!

Wealthy, powerful, gorgeous men...
Women who have feelings just like your own...
The stories you love, set in exotic, glamorous locations...

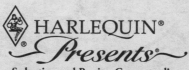

HARLEQUIN®
Presents

Seduction and Passion Guaranteed!

HPDIR08

www.eHarlequin.com

Harlequin® Historical
Historical Romantic Adventure!

Imagine a time of chivalrous knights and unconventional ladies, roguish rakes and impetuous heiresses, rugged cowboys and spirited frontierswomen—— these rich and vivid tales will capture your imagination!

Harlequin Historical . . . they're too good to miss!

SPECIAL EDITION™

*Emotional, compelling stories that capture the intensity of
living, loving and creating a family in today's world.*

Modern, passionate reads that are powerful and provocative.

n o c t u r n e

Dramatic and sensual tales of paranormal romance.

Romances that are sparked by danger and fueled by passion.